Armada Quest

PATHFINDER
SERIES

Armada Quest

IRENE WAY

ZONDERVAN
PUBLISHING HOUSE
OF THE ZONDERVAN CORPORATION
GRAND RAPIDS, MICHIGAN 49506

ARMADA QUEST
Copyright © PICKERING & INGLIS LTD. 1976

Published in 1976

Published by Zondervan Publishing House in the USA by special arrangement with Pickering and Inglis Ltd. of London and Glasgow.

Zondervan Edition 1979

Library of Congress Cataloging in Publication Data

Way, Irene.
    Armada quest.

(Pathfinder series)
    SUMMARY: Newly moved to a Scottish island, a pair of twins runs into danger as they race with a thief to solve the mystery of the lost treasure ship, the San Salvador.
    [1.   Mystery and detective stories.
2.   Scotland—Fiction]   I.   Title.   II.   Series:
Pathfinder series (Grand Rapids)
PZ7.W3512Ar 1979   [Fic]   78-26401
ISBN 0-310-37841-9

Printed in the United States of America

CONTENTS

THE SPANISH ARMADA

An armada (ar-MAH-da) is a fleet of armed ships. The Spanish Armada, also called the "Invincible Armada," consisted of about 130 sailing ships. It was sent by King Philip II of Spain in the summer of 1588 to invade and conquer England.

The Spanish Armada and the English Navy had several battles, beginning with one off the coast of Plymouth, England, and followed by others farther north in the English Channel (between England and the rest of Europe). The "Invincible Armada" was defeated by the English Navy, which had more ships and stronger guns.

Only a few of the ships in the Spanish Armada were destroyed in battle. The rest limped northward around the tip of Scotland. The ships were in poor condition, and many of them sank or were wrecked on the rocky shores. Only about half of the original number made it back to Spain.

1

Welcome to Benlarich

Jonathan Mackenzie leaned over the bow of the S.S. *Lochaber* and pointed excitedly into the distance.

"Look, Jo, there it is!"

His sister moved closer to him and, shading her eyes against the bright sunshine, stared at the faint smudge on the horizon. The strong breeze ruffled their curly auburn hair as they stood shoulder to shoulder against the rail, so alike in height and features that it was obvious to everyone that they were twins.

"I wonder how long before we get in," she said. "I can't wait to see our new home."

"I thought perhaps you were feeling seasick," said Jon teasingly. "The sea's a little on the rough side, isn't it? I've never been so far on a boat before."

Joanna made a face. "To think that we have to make this trip each time we leave the island. That's the worst part of it."

"Still," said Jon, "perhaps if the weather's bad, we won't be able to get back to school. That could be fun!"

On hearing Jon's excited call, Mr. and Mrs. Mackenzie came out from the forward cabin to get their first view of the island that was to be their new home.

Mrs. Mackenzie shivered suddenly in spite of the warm sunshine.

"I do hope we're doing the right thing, dear," she said. "It's a big step to take, pulling up roots and moving from the south of England to the Western Isles."

"Of course it's the right step, Myra," said Andrew Mackenzie confidently. "We prayed about it, and we believe that God wants us to make this move. Perhaps he has work for us here. Who knows?"

It was difficult even now to realize that only six weeks ago they had never thought of living on the island of Benlarich off the west coast of Scotland. Then had come that amazing letter from a firm of lawyers in Glasgow, informing Mr. Mackenzie that his uncle, Hamish Mackenzie, had died and left his estate on Benlarich to Andrew on the condition that the family would make their permanent home there.

For Andrew Mackenzie there had been no decision to make. As a writer he could work anywhere, and to settle on a small Scottish island certainly appealed to his sense of adventure. His wife had not been quite so easy to convince, but the delight and enthusiasm of the twins soon won her over.

Now they were almost there, and the family watched with suppressed excitement—and perhaps apprehension—as the island gradually drew nearer.

* * * * * * *

Jon watched anxiously as their luggage was unloaded onto the dock. His father checked to see that everything had arrived safely, then looked around for someone to direct them to their new home.

An interested group of local islanders had watched the docking, and were now waving as the steamer slowly pulled away from the wharf. Jon suddenly felt as if his last link with the life he had known was finally and completely severed.

A man was pushing his way through the crowd, and stopped breathlessly in front of Mr. Mackenzie.

"Sorry I wasn't here when you arrived, sir. I'm Jamie Sinclair, manager for the estate. I've brought the carriage to take you all up to the house."

Jon stared admiringly at the handsome young Scot in his kilt and purse, with a dagger thrust into the top of his thick sock.

"A carriage!" gasped Joanna, unbelievingly. "Not —not a horse-drawn carriage?"

"Aye. It's only a wee one, but Mr. Hamish took to using it quite a bit in the last days when he couldn't get around so well. It's way up on the road there."

Jamie pointed over the heads of the bystanders to where a smart horse and carriage were waiting. Picking up the hand luggage, Jon and Joanna, followed by Mrs. Mackenzie, walked quickly towards it, leaving their father and Jamie to cope with the heavier suitcases.

The horse, a beautiful well-groomed bay, neighed softly as the twins rushed around to stroke his nose.

Soon all the suitcases were safely stored in the carriage, and the Mackenzie family took their seats, Jon choosing to ride in front with Jamie.

"Isn't 'San Salvador' a strange name for a house on a Scottish island, Jamie? What made Great-Uncle Hamish call it that, I wonder?"

"It was no' your Great-Uncle who named the house,

3

Master Jon. It was built nearly four hundred years ago—the original that is—and has been added to since. Legend has it that one of the Armada ships, named *San Salvador*, was wrecked in these waters in 1588. That's probably where the name came from."

"The Spanish Armada! Do you think a treasure ship could be sunk in the bay—like at Tobermory?"

Jamie laughed loudly, flinging his dark, curly head back and opening his mouth wide, so that the sound poured out into the quiet around them.

"So you're on the treasure trail already, Master Jon."

Jon gasped and grabbed Jamie's arm so suddenly that he was almost dislodged from his seat.

"Do you mean—do you mean there really is Spanish treasure in the bay?"

Jamie's sun-tanned face crinkled with amusement at the boy's enthusiasm.

"There's always been rumors about a treasure ship. My father was manager before me, and my mother has been housekeeper at 'San Salvador' for many years. They both remember hearing the story when they were young. When I was a lad, we used to explore the island, looking for clues, but nothing has ever been found—not to my knowledge anyway. Get up there, Major!"

The horse's gait quickened as the lane wound slowly down into a beautiful sheltered valley, completely circled by high wooded hills, and with its own clean, white, sandy beach. On the hillside stood a large house, surrounded by well-kept lawns and rose gardens.

Mrs. Mackenzie half rose from her seat. "That's

4

never the house, is it, Jamie? Not that huge place!" she exclaimed.

"Aye, ma'am, that's 'San Salvador,' and the farms lie on the other side of yon hill."

The Mackenzie family was speechless with amazement at the size and extent of their inheritance. With an amused smile on his face, Jamie urged Major up the private road leading to the house. In a matter of minutes, the carriage was easing to a standstill in front of the large, iron-studded door, and Jon jumped down excitedly.

"Wow, Dad! What a place! It's fit for a king to live in!"

The others quickly climbed out of the carriage and followed Jon up the stone steps.

"Hey! Look at this, everybody!"

Jon pointed to a piece of paper fastened to the door. The letters were large and crudely written, but the meaning was unmistakable.

YOU ARE NOT WANTED HERE. GO AWAY NOW, OR THE CURSE OF THE SPANIARD WILL FALL UPON YOU.

Mrs. Mackenzie gasped. "Oh, Andrew, what does it mean?"

Mr. Mackenzie looked grim. "It means, my dear, that someone is trying to scare us away. Come on, ring the bell, Jon. This wants looking into."

The sound of the bell echoed through the house, and the Mackenzie family stood uneasily on the step, waiting—and wondering what the future held in store for them at "San Salvador."

5

2

The First Clue
to the Mystery

A few mornings later, when Jo woke up, the sky was a glorious blue with just a spattering of fleecy white clouds.

She took out her Bible, and turned to the story of Jesus preaching from the boat on the Sea of Galilee. "It must have been a beautiful day just like this," she thought. "Oh, Jesus, I do thank You for bringing us to this lovely place. Show me how I can use my life to serve You."

A knock on the door told her Jon was ready, so they hurried down to breakfast and then went to play on the grounds.

They were called in, some time later, by a shout from Jamie. "Come along, Jon and Joanna. Your father wants you in the study."

"What does he want?" muttered Jon, idly kicking a stone into the ornamental goldfish pond. "We can't have done anything wrong yet—we haven't had time."

Joanna laughed. "Come on, silly. I expect he just wants to tell us something."

In the study, their parents were standing looking out through the window, across the wooded valley to where the slopes of Benlarich, which gave the island its name, rose stark and bare to the sky.

Andrew Mackenzie turned as the door opened, and his handsome, rugged face creased into a smile as he saw the twins.

"Ah! There you are. Been exploring the grounds?"

"Yes, Dad," said Jon, "it's terrific. Trees to climb, woods to play in, beaches, and caves—but we haven't been down there yet."

"Well, you deserve some fun," said their mother. "You have been working hard these last few days, helping us to sort everything out. But please be careful. You don't know the island yet, you know."

There was a knock on the door.

"Come in," called Mr. Mackenzie.

The door opened, and in came the housekeeper, Mrs. Sinclair, a short, plump, gray-haired figure in a black dress and starched white apron, followed by her son, Jamie.

"Thank you for coming. Do sit down a moment." They seated themselves, and looked expectantly at Mr. Mackenzie.

"We are a little disturbed by the message we found fastened to the front door when we arrived," said Mr. Mackenzie. "I wondered whether you can throw any light on it."

Mrs. Sinclair shook her head. "Perhaps it's just a stupid practical joke, sir."

"Can you think of anyone who has any reason for not wanting us here? As far as I know, I was Uncle Hamish's only relative—I know of no one else who could have expected to inherit."

"That's right, sir," Jamie agreed. "Mr. Hamish always told us that the estate would go to you."

"Perhaps it's got something to do with the treasure, Dad," burst in Jon.

"What treasure?" His mother looked surprised.

"The Spanish treasure ship that was wrecked here. Jamie told me about it in the carriage."

"Is there a treasure ship?" asked Mr. Mackenzie.

Jamie laughed. "You know how it is, sir. These legends persist, and no one quite knows where they started. It has always been said that one of the Armada galleons was wrecked off this island—*San Salvador*—which gave the name to the house. As far as I know, nothing has ever been found—no parts of a ship, no cannon, no treasure—but that doesn't stop people looking."

Mrs. Mackenzie looked startled. "Do you mean that people actually come here to search for this treasure ship?"

"Oh yes, ma'am. Every year brings its crop of explorers—the genuine historians who are following up old legends or manuscripts, and the fortune hunters, just out for some fun."

There was complete silence for a few moments. Then Mr. Mackenzie asked Jamie quietly, "Have either you or your mother any reason to believe that Uncle Hamish might have found something? Some clue, perhaps, which he passed on to someone else?"

Mrs. Sinclair shook her head. "Mr. Hamish was never one to chatter, Mr. Andrew. If he had come across something, I doubt he would have said anything to us."

8

"Had he any close friends on the island with whom he might have shared a secret?" asked Mr. Mackenzie.

"Aye, that he had," said Jamie. "His old school friend, Dr. Gordon from the village, and Alistair Mac-Bride from the Folly were here every week. If anyone would know, it could be one of them."

"Perhaps I'll give them a call and invite them to dinner tonight. Then we can have a chat," said Mr. Mackenzie.

"Were you with Uncle Hamish when he died?" Mrs. Mackenzie asked the housekeeper.

"Aye. He had been poorly for several days, and the guid doctor had prescribed some tablets for the pain, but the end came more quickly than we expected, and he slipped away quite peacefully in his sleep," she explained.

"If he knew that he hadn't long to live," said Mr. Mackenzie slowly, "then it's quite possible that he has left some clue to what he had found—if anything."

The twins stared at their father, and it was Joanna who found her tongue first.

"Do you really think that Great-Uncle Hamish found something, Dad?"

"Possibly—I don't know. I suppose he left no letter for me when he died, Mrs. Sinclair?"

"No, sir. All his papers were in the deed box at the bank, and the lawyer took charge of those. Of course, there is his desk in the library—all that was left for you to attend to, sir."

"Then that might account for . . . ." Jamie stopped abruptly.

"For what?" prompted Mr. Mackenzie.

9

"Well, it may be nothing at all, Mr. Andrew, but just after Mr. Hamish died, I found the library window open and a lot of papers all over the floor. I assumed that the wind had blown them about, but it is possible that it was a . . . ."

"Burglar!" shouted the twins excitedly.

Their mother looked horrified, and there was a pause while they digested this latest piece of news.

"Well, until we know more," said Mr. Mackenzie quietly, "I think we should all be on our guard. Let me know about anything unusual you see or hear, and please be particularly careful about locking up at night."

Mrs. Sinclair nodded and rose from her chair.

"Oh, and by the way," Mr. Mackenzie went on, "please don't say anything about this in the village. It may be just a practical joke after all."

The housekeeper and her son left, and the twins started to follow.

"Just a moment, you two," said their father. "Make sure you always tell someone where you're going if you leave the grounds. I know we believe Jesus is looking after us wherever we are and whatever we are doing, but the forces of evil are very strong, and we should take every precaution until this matter is cleared up."

Mrs. Mackenzie looked anxious. "You don't really thing there's any danger, do you, Andrew?"

He smiled. "Not really, dear, but it's better to be safe than sorry. Off you go, then."

*   *   *   *   *   *   *

The twins needed no second bidding. They raced

outside and down to the shrubbery which shielded one side of the house. There were garden seats placed here and there, and selecting one which gave an excellent view of the bay, the twins sat down.

"Well," said Jon, "where shall we start?"

"Start what?"

"Looking for the treasure, of course. I'm sure, Great-Uncle Hamish found something, and he must have left us a clue. The point is, where?"

"But why didn't he just leave a letter for Dad, or something like that?"

"Perhaps he thought someone was after it, and the first thing they'd do would be to search his papers."

"Then you think it really was a burglar who got into the house, Jon?"

"Certainly seems like it. That's why I'm sure there was something to hide—and we've just got to find it."

"But it could be anywhere—in the house, or even a secret hideway in the grounds. It would take years to search everywhere."

"Then we've got to size up the whole situation logically, and go through it step by step," said Jon, importantly. "Tell you what, let's have a good old game in the grounds now, and then after lunch, we'll go up to my room and plan our campaign. The weather looks as if it might blow up rough later, anyway, so let's make the most of it while we can."

"Good idea," agreed Joanna, and the two raced off through the shrubbery to a small woods which looked ideal for a game of hide-and-seek.

"I'll hide first, Jo. Give me up to fifty," shouted Jon, and disappeared into the trees.

Joanna began to count—not *too* slowly—and then shouting "Coming," she, too, moved into the woods, her sharp eyes searching the ground for signs of Jon. A broken branch on a nearby bush and a footprint in a soft piece of ground quickly indicated the path he had taken. But after Joanna reached higher, drier ground, her task became more difficult. She stopped and listened, hoping that Jon would give himself away. But she heard nothing. She moved on slowly, singing softly to herself—

"Living He loved me, dying He saved me,
Buried, He carried my sins far away,
Rising He justified, freely forever,
One day He's coming, oh glorious day!"

She searched all the likely spots, then suddenly a twig snapped behind her—like a pistol shot.

"Caught you!" she cried as she turned around—and then recoiled in horror.

Facing her, and looking almost as surprised as she felt, was a stranger. Turning on his heel, he ran into the trees and disappeared.

"Jon!" she shrieked. "Jon! Come quickly!"

"What's the matter?" asked Jon, running towards her from a nearby thicket.

"Oh, Jon," gasped Joanna, grabbing his arm, "I heard a noise and I thought it was you. But it was a man—big and dark, with a black beard. He turned and ran away. Oh, I was frightened."

"I'm sure you were," said Jon, sympathetically, "but he wasn't expecting to see you either—that's why he ran. Let's have a look around."

Jon searched the area, and a few seconds later shouted excitedly, "Here—look at this, Jo."

Under a rocky overhang someone had made a rough campsite. There were a couple of tin cans, bits of paper, and the ashes of a fire. "Nobody here now," muttered Jon, "but there certainly has been." He poked about for a few minutes, and then noticed a piece of paper caught between the rocks.

"What have you found, Jon?" asked Joanna, peering over his shoulder.

"Something important enough to be burned," Jon answered. "See, the edges have been scorched, but it looks as though the wind blew it away before it caught properly."

"What does it say? Can you read it?"

"There's only a few words left. Look!" and he passed her the paper.

> ome as soon as y
> mily arrived but they ha
> thing. We must search fo
> iary. Perhaps a secret hi
> the house. Take ca
> en. Will meet you
> ish Oak.
> Mi

"Let's take it home and study it there, Jon." Joanna shivered slightly. "I'm frightened that man might come back."

"Good idea, Jo. Come on."

13

They hurried away, Joanna looking fearfully around her as they ran.

* * * * * * *

By the time the twins got back to the house, they found it was almost lunch time.

"The morning's gone quickly, and I'm absolutely starving," exclaimed Joanna.

"Me, too," Jon admitted. "By the way, Jo, don't say anything about the letter—or that man—until we've had a chance to discuss it."

At that moment their mother came into the room. "Hello, you two. I was wondering where you were. Have you seen your father anywhere? Oh, there you are, Andrew," as Mr. Mackenzie came in through the door. "Mrs. Sinclair is ready to serve."

The silence with which they ate was a tribute to the excellence of Mrs. Sinclair's cooking, and it wasn't until the dessert course—a delicious peach Melba—that Mr. Mackenzie asked, "What have you two been doing all morning? I haven't had sight or sound of you."

"Oh, we've been exploring, Dad. Through the shrubbery and over to the woods. It's lovely there. We had a good game of hide-and-seek.

Mr. Mackenzie looked serious. "Jamie tells me that someone has been seen prowling in the grounds. Until we know who he is or what he's up to, I'd rather you didn't go too far afield without telling us."

The twins exchanged glances. "Right, Dad, we'll remember that," said Jon. "Have you finished, Jo? Let's go upstairs. Excuse us, please."

Mr. Mackenzie nodded, and watched them curiously as they went out.

"Do you think they've seen anything, Andrew?"

"So you noticed it, too," their father said, thoughtfully. "They're up to something—I'm sure of it."

* * * * * * *

Up in his small, pleasantly furnished bedroom, looking out over the sea, Jon pulled two chairs up to the table and spread out the piece of paper they had found.

"It shouldn't be too difficult to make sense of it," he said, taking a notebook from the shelf. "Let's see what we can get."

"Well, the first line must be 'Come as soon as you. . . ,'"

"The rest is really difficult," grumbled Jo. "Write out all you can and see what it looks like now."

Starting a fresh sheet, Jon carefully printed out the words:

> COME AS SOON AS YOU
> FAMILY ARRIVED BUT THEY HAVE
> THING. WE MUST SEARCH FOR
> DIARY. PERHAPS A SECRET HI
> THE HOUSE. TAKE CA
> EN. WILL MEET YOU
> ISH OAK.
> MI

"That looks more promising," Jon said.

"What do you think 'blank, blank, blank, blank-ISH OAK' means in the last line?" Joanna asked.

"Could be 'Spanish Oak,'" said Jon. "Everything seems to be Spanish around here. And that word beginning with 'HI' is probably 'hideout' or 'hiding place.' I should think the next line is 'Take care not to be seen.'"

"Yes, I expect you're right. The point is, who sent it? And who is the stranger we saw?"

"Your guess is as good as mine. This house is full of hiding places—we could look forever and not find anything. Could even be full of sliding panels, hidden passages, secret rooms—everything!"

"But surely Jamie or his mother would know if anything like that is possible."

"I should think so. Anyway, we must see him as soon as we can and find out if there is a Spanish Oak. It could be important."

Just then there was a brilliant flash of lightning, followed immediately by a colossal thunderclap.

"Oh dear," groaned Joanna, "we're going to have a storm. That puts an end to our exploring outside this afternoon."

Jon had moved across to the window which gave a view of the sea beyond the shrubbery and woods.

"Jo! Quick!" he called.

His sister rushed across to join him.

"There," he cried, pointing towards the trees. "Look there!"

The rain was now bucketing down, which made it difficult to see, but Joanna could just make out a figure hurrying into the shelter of the trees.

"It's him!" she gasped. "I'm sure it's the same man I saw this morning. I recognize the checked shirt he's wearing!"

3

An Intruder Calls Twice

Later that night, Jon tapped gently on Joanna's bedroom door. When there was no answer, he tapped again, then turned the handle and went in. He stopped short when he saw his sister on her knees by the side of the bed.

"What are you doing down there, Jo?" he inquired. "Have you lost something?"

"No, I haven't lost anything," Jo replied, quietly. "I was just saying my prayers."

Jon stared disbelievingly. "Prayers!" he echoed. "I didn't think you still believed in that rubbish, Jo!"

Jo got to her feet slowly, drawing her robe more closely around her. "It isn't rubbish, Jon. We've always been brought up to go to church and to say our prayers. You'd better not let Mom and Dad hear you talk like that. They'd be upset."

"I don't care. I don't mind going to church with you and all that, but I don't have to believe it, do I?" Jon flung himself down in an armchair, and began to whistle tunelessly.

Joanna sat on the edge of the bed and looked at her twin as if seeing him for the first time.

17

"But what about Jesus? Don't you believe in Him, in what He did for us? His life is a historical fact, and you can't deny a fact, can you! Besides, don't you have to attend prayers and church when you're at your boarding school? Surely they don't let you just stay away?"

Jon looked uncomfortable. "Oh no. We have to go to them all right. But some of us have had discussions about it, and we've decided that there can't be any truth in it. Stands to reason, doesn't it, when you really think about it? As if someone could die and come to life again. Ha! If you believe that, you'll believe anything."

Joanna felt her cheeks flushing. "Thousands of people have died for that belief, anyway," she said, quietly.

"More fool they, then," said Jon loftily. "Better to live for adventure and excitement than believing in a silly old fairy tale!"

"Oh, Jon! How can you say such wicked things! Jesus died to save us from our sins. No one can make a greater sacrifice than to give up his life for someone else. Don't you want to go to heaven and enjoy all the wonderful things Jesus is preparing for us? Besides, life isn't worth living at all if you don't have faith in something."

"I'd sooner have faith in myself. How can you believe all the fantastic stories in the Bible, like the Flood, the Walls of Jericho, the Fiery Furnace, and the miracles? If one thing isn't true, then it's probably all not true. Why I. . . ."

"Listen, Jon! I thought I heard a noise."

"You're changing the subject because you know you're losing an argument," Jon grumbled.

"No, seriously, Jon. I thought I heard something

downstairs—in the library. Perhaps it's the burglar again."

"We'll soon find out. Wait while I go and get my flashlight." Jon rose quietly to his feet and slipped into his own roon, returning a few seconds later with a flashlight in his hand. Signaling to Jo, he led the way to the top of the old oak staircase. "Be careful of the third step from the bottom," Jo warned. "It creaks."

Quietly and carefully the twins crept downstairs, avoiding the third step as they passed. A thin line of light showed under the lounge door where their parents were still entertaining Dr. Gordon and Mr. MacBride.

Joanna tugged at his sleeve. "Perhaps it was just Mrs. Sinclair we heard," she whispered. "The guests haven't left yet, so she will still be in the kitchen."

"Could be," said Jon, "but I think we'll just take a quick look. It's bound to be the library—that's where he tried before."

Creeping towards the library door, Jon grasped the handle and turned it gently.

"Don't you think we ought to call Father?" Joanna whispered, timidly. "Just in case it is a burglar!"

"Nonsense!" answered her brother, firmly. "I can deal with this."

The door opened quietly on its well-oiled hinges, and the twins stepped into the huge library. They could hear a scuffling sound from the corner where the diffused glow from a small hurricane lamp clearly outlined the large oak desk and the wall panelling behind. Jon dug Joanna in the ribs with his elbow and pointed. The desk was in a terrible mess, with papers pulled from the pigeonholes and strewn all over the floor. A shadowy figure was standing behind the desk, carefully feeling the fine oak panelling which made up the walls of the library.

"It must be here," they heard the intruder mutter to himself.

He worked on silently for a few moments, and then there was a sharp click. A section of the panelling slid back to reveal a dark opening. With a low cry of triumph, the man turned and seized the lamp to investigate his find. Jon grabbed his sister's arm to draw her back into the shadows, but it was too late. As the man lifted the lamp, its rays clearly outlined the two figures near the door.

"So," he said quietly. "It is my little friend from the woods."

Then, with a sudden movement of his hand, he turned down the wick in the lamp. There was a confused blur of sound as the panelling slid shut, and the man made a dash for the French windows. It was only seconds before the twins followed him. There was a crash as Jon toppled over a chair, followed by a mocking laugh from the window as the intruder raced away towards the woods.

Suddenly the library lights were switched on, and the twins, momentarily blinded, turned to see their parents and the visitors standing in the doorway, staring in bewilderment.

"Just what is going on in here?" asked Mr. Mackenzie. "And what are you doing out of bed?"

"It was the burglar again, Dad," said Jon, excitedly.

"We heard a noise and came down to investigate. . . ." Joanna went on.

". . . and found him examining the panelling behind the desk," Jon interrupted. "He found a secret switch and a panel opened. That's when he saw us, so he put out his lamp, closed the panel, and ran away. We were too late to stop him."

"Just as well," said Dr. Gordon. "He might have attacked you."

Joanna shuddered.

"I was just telling your father that someone's been asking questions around the village," Dr. Gordon went on. "A man had a room at Widow Thomson's for several weeks before Hamish died, but then he paid his bill and left, and we assumed that he had gone from the island. It could be the same man. He might have holed out in a cave somewhere."

Mr. Mackenzie had been examining the window frame carefully. "Broken the lock," he said at last. "I'll have to get Jamie to fix a new one tomorrow."

"But he might come back tonight," said Joanna. "He found the secret hideout, but he didn't have time to see what was inside. He's bound to come back."

"Aye, he is that," said Mr. MacBride, pulling at his gray, bushy moustache as he spoke. "So you must be ready for him next time. I'd suggest, Andrew, that you ask yon Jamie Sinclair to sleep in the library from now on."

"That I will," said Mr. Mackenzie, nodding in agreement. "Come into the lounge, children, and hear what Dr. Gordon has been telling us about Uncle Hamish."

They all went into the lounge and settled themselves comfortably. A few minutes later, Mrs. Sinclair brought in a tray of coffee and thickly buttered scones and scotch pancakes.

When the coffee had been poured, Dr. Gordon stretched his gaunt frame in the armchair, ran his long thin fingers through his sparse gray hair, and began speaking quietly.

"Ye didna ken Hamish, I gather, else ye'd know he was a rare, obstinate body, afeared of no one and a law unto himself." He smiled across at Jon and Joanna who were leaning forward listening intently. His bright blue eyes twinkled as he sensed their barely concealed excitement.

"When the rumors started again about the Spanish treasure ship, I tackled Hamish about it, but he was in a rare temper that night, so I didn't press the subject, thinking it best to wait until he chose to tell me. That he had found something I was absolutely certain."

"Aye," agreed Alistair MacBride, "he was an awful close man. He wouldna admit tae anything. I ken well the night he brought out those three gold coins. He said he'd found them in the sand near the headland. They were Spanish pieces of eight."

Dr. Gordon nodded. "When he was fast coming to the end of the road, he sent for us both late one night, and it was then he admitted that he'd found the treasure."

There were gasps of disbelief from the twins, and even their parents leaned forward with interest.

"Did he. . . ." Mrs. Mackenzie began.

"Aye," Dr. Gordon said slowly. "He said that he had left a letter for you, Andrew, giving you a clue to its whereabouts, but. . . ." There was a pause, and Dr. Gordon stared at each member of the party in turn. "He was afraid to explain too many details because he believed that someone else was after it. He quoted the words of Jesus, 'Lay not up treasure for yourselves on earth. . .' and said he believed God had a special use for this treasure, and he didn't want it to get into the wrong hands. He had received a threatening letter saying that a curse would fall on him if the treasure was not handed over."

"Did Hamish tell you where he left the letter?" asked Mr. Mackenzie.

Alistair MacBride looked surprised. "He didn't say exactly. Haven't you found it?"

"No, I haven't," Mr. Mackenzie replied in a worried tone. "I should have thought he would have left it with the lawyer, or perhaps in his desk, but I've found nothing."

"Perhaps the burglar found it after all," Joanna volunteered.

"It doesn't appear so, else why is he still searching?" her father pointed out.

Dr. Gordon cleared his throat noisily. "Perhaps I can make a suggestion," he said. "The letter is sure to be in the house somewhere; I canna see Hamish giving the letter to anyone else, not even his lawyer. He was not a trusting man, and he liked to be mysterious. I reckon he's hidden the letter, and he knew that when we told you about the treasure, you'd turn the house upside down until you found it. Also, it wouldn't be anywhere obvious—especially if he thought someone else was after it."

"That's true," Jon admitted. "When do we start looking?"

"Not tonight, that's for sure," said his mother, briskly. "Off to bed with you now, Joanna, Jon. We'll discuss it again at breakfast tomorrow."

"Don't do anything without us, will you, Dad?" said Jon anxiously.

There was a loud guffaw from Mr. MacBride. "Dinna fash yersel', laddie, there'll be plenty for you to do!"

"For us all to do," said Mr. Mackenzie, grimly. "Off to bed with you now."

* * * * * * *

The twins were up bright and early the next morning, even though the sky was overcast. Breakfast was a lively meal. Mrs. Sinclair was bustling in and out of the kitchen, and Jamie had already started on his day's work.

Jon helped himself to his fifth slice of toast, and asked cheerfully, "Well, Dad, what's the plan? Where are we going to start?"

"That, my son, is the sixty-four dollar question," said his father, stirring his coffee. "In my opinion there's no point in searching outside, for Hamish wasn't at all active towards the end, and it's hardly likely the letter will be hidden outside. So, it's the house we'll concentrate on."

"The library's the place," Joanna added. "Jon and I can try to find that secret panel."

"Good idea, Jo." agreed her brother. "Dad can come and help us when he's free."

"If you go then," said Mrs. Mackenzie. "I'll come and help you, too, just as soon as I've had a

24

word with Mrs. Sinclair about today's meal."

Jon and Joanna rose quickly from the table and began stacking the dishes on the nearby teacart. Suddenly, they heard a loud scream from the kitchen, followed by a crash. After a stunned silence Mr. Mackenzie rushed for the door, closely followed by his wife and the twins. It took only seconds to reach the kitchen door and fling it open.

Mr. Mackenzie stepped back in surprise. Mrs. Sinclair was lying full length on the floor, unconscious. Fastened to the pine kitchen table by a wicked-looking dagger was a scrawled note.

> YOU DID NOT HEED MY WARNING. NEXT TIME YOU MAY NOT BE SO LUCKY. THE CURSE OF THE SPANIARD WILL FALL SOON.

"Is she all right?" asked Mrs. Mackenzie, bending over the still form anxiously.

"I think she's only fainted," said her husband. "But this joke has gone far enough. I'm going to call the police!"

4
Disappointment and Danger

"Poor Mrs. Sinclair," said Joanna, as she and her brother went into the library some time later. "I do hope she will be all right."

"Oh, I should think so," said Jon, airily. "Dr. Gordon said it was only a faint, and she looks perfectly O.K. now."

"Must have been the shock of seeing that fellow sticking the note to the table that made her faint."

"Probably," Jon agreed, "but now that Dad's told the police about it, they're keeping an eye open for him."

"I hope they catch him soon. He might be really nasty if he was cornered. And all those threats about the 'Curse of the Spaniard.'"

"Better say your prayers regularly, Jo, so that nothing happens to you," mocked Jon, with a broad grin.

Joanna felt her cheeks flush, but she was determined not to let Jon make her angry.

"You scoff as much as you like, Jon," she said, with quiet dignity. "I believe that Jesus *will* look after me if I trust Him. As it happens, I have said a prayer for our safety—all of us, and I know that Mom and

26

Dad had prayer together just now."

"Come on," said Jon suddenly, "let's get on with our search for the secret panel."

The panelling in the library was of dark oak, and beautifully carved in a most artistic design of flowers, leaves, and acorns. It reached about five feet high, with plain oak panels above this reaching to the ceiling, which, by virtue of their plainness, seemed to emphasize the delicate tracery of the carving below. For a few moments the twins stood examining the design.

"One thing," said Joanna, at length, "thanks to our enemy—Gonzales, I think Mr. MacBride said that man called himself—we do know roughly where to look. It would have taken us a long time to try all around."

"It sure would," agreed Jon. "Tell you what—you start on that side of the desk and I'll start on this side, and we'll work towards each other. We know it must be within this area."

They began to press, pull, turn, or slide each of the designs on the woodwork, but after half an hour's unsuccessful twiddling, Jon threw himself down in a chair in disgust.

"We're getting nowhere," he complained bitterly, "yet we know there's a hidden opening there."

"Gonzales only found it by accident," Joanna pointed out, "so it can't be too complicated a mechanism. It's just a question of finding the right knob—there's so many of them." She stopped as she spoke and examined the panelling closely. "Look, Jon," she called, presently, "this motif here is very slightly different from the others. Perhaps it's a clue."

Jon jumped to his feet and joined her. She pointed to a cluster of acorns and oak leaves, and sure enough, the design of the leaves did differ slightly—but only very slightly—from the rest of the panel.

"You did well to spot that," said Jon, admiringly. "I'd never have noticed it in a million years."

Joanna began to press the acorn with her fingers, and seconds later there was a click and the panel slid open.

"What did you do?" asked Jon.

"I turned the acorn to the left. I expect you turn it to the right to close it."

Jon patted her on the back. "Good show, Jo. I'll get a flashlight and tell Mom and Dad we've found it. Don't go in there without me."

Joanna smiled. Jon didn't like to be left out of anything.

Hurrying footsteps indicated the excited arrival of Mr. and Mrs. Mackenzie. "Good work, you two," said their father. "Have you got your flashlight, Jon?"

"Yes, here you are, Dad."

Mr. Mackenzie bowed dramatically. "To you intrepid explorers must go the privilege of being the first to enter."

The twins laughed, but Jon was quickly inside and shining his flashlight around. The room was small and sparsely furnished with a table, a chair, and a small corner sink which could be used for washing. A luxurious carpet covered the floor, and the walls were panelled in similar style to the library.

"Wow!" said Jon. "A secret room! But the air is perfectly pure."

"Obviously there's an air duct concealed some-

28

where," Mrs. Mackenzie commented. "This house could well be a regular rabbit warren of hidden rooms and tunnels."

Jon had been looking around the walls and turned his attention to the table. This was small but heavy, and again exquisitely carved. He examined it carefully, and the others clustered around at his sudden gasp of excitement.

"Look, Dad! Here's a very tiny keyhole. There must be a drawer inside, though it's beautifully concealed."

Mr. Mackenzie reached into his trouser pocket and produced Great-Uncle Hamish's bunch of keys. He selected a tiny, silver key and inserted it into the lock.

"So that's what that tiny one is for," he said.

The lock turned easily, and a center panel in the table slid open. The cavity was empty save for a small envelope. Mr. Mackenzie took it and in the half light, read his own name on the letter.

"Uncle Hamish's letter," he said with a smile. "Let's adjourn to the library and see what he has to say."

The twins needed no second bidding, and were soon seated around the library table, the room behind them sealed once more.

Mr. Mackenzie carefully opened the letter and drew out a single sheet of paper.

"He doesn't intend to tell us much," he commented drily.

The writing was small and neat, though obviously that of an elderly person. Mr. Mackenzie began to read:

"My dear nephew,
    "I'm sorry that it has not been possible for us

to meet and to get to know one another. It is my own fault that I have cut myself off from the family, and I have paid for my foolishness. Recently, I made a great discovery which I kept to myself, not even sharing it with my good friends, Dr. Gordon and Alistair MacBride. Now it is too late. I know I haven't long to live, and my discovery will die with me. I know someone is spying on me to steal my secret, so I cannot risk leaving any clues.

"So, my dear Andrew, my apologies to you and your family. I hope you enjoy living at 'San Salvador.' Please love the house as I have loved it, and cherish it for my sake.

"My love to you all, and may the good Lord in whom I have always trusted richly bless you.

Hamish Mackenzie

"P.S. You will find some interesting historical facts about the original *San Salvador* in the *Great Armada* by J.R. Hale which I commend to your attention."

There was complete silence as Mr. Mackenzie finished reading the letter. Then Jon exploded. "Well! What a sell! The mean old codger—now we shall never find the treasure."

His father frowned. "That's quite enough, Jon. If Uncle Hamish was being threatened, then he was quite right not to commit the secret to paper. That's what that scoundrel was looking for, for certain."

"Now that we're living here, we have just as much chance of solving the mystery as Uncle Hamish had," said Mrs. Mackenzie, peaceably.

"Some hopes," grumbled Jon. "We don't even know where to start."

"Well, I'm going to start by reading the book that Great-Uncle Hamish has mentioned," said Joanna with determination. "Come and help me find it, Jon."

* * * * * * *

Lunch was a dismal meal. Mr. and Mrs. Mackenzie tried to keep the conversation going, but found it difficult. Joanna seemed wrapped in her own thoughts, while Jon was definitely sulky. Mr. Mackenzie shook his head slowly and smiled across at his wife.

"Come on, Jon," he said, "Snap out of it. This is a challenge, not a disaster. Jesus told us, 'Seek and ye shall find.' Suppose we apply His advice to the present situation?"

"But Dad—" Jon protested. "How do we know where to start looking? Surely Great-Uncle could have left us some clue."

"Perhaps he has," said Joanna, looking her brother straight in the eye. "Perhaps we're just too stupid to see it."

"Let's give it a rest," said her father, hurriedly. "Say, what about trying the boat out this afternoon? The weather's cleared up beautifully, and I'd like to see the other side of the island, wouldn't you?"

Even Jon brightened up at that. "Oh, yes, Dad," he said. "That would be super. D'you really mean it?"

"Sure do," said his father, with a grin. "Come on now, what are you both waiting for?"

* * * * * * *

The little sailing boat—*Bonny Prince*—pranced about

31

on the water as the gusty breeze billowed the sail. Jon held the tiller while his father saw to the sail. Joanna sat in the bow, watching the rocky coastline. Mr. Mackenzie looked at them both with pride. This move to Scotland was the best thing that could have happened—and he gave thanks to God for helping them to make the right decision.

Joanna was gazing at the beauty around her, but her heart was sad. "How can I explain to Jon just what loving Jesus means to me?" she thought. "I couldn't start the day without asking Jesus to bless me and watch over me, and I certainly couldn't go to bed without asking His forgiveness for the mistakes I've made during the day. What can I do to help Jon?" She closed her eyes and her heart sent up a fervent prayer for help to find the right words to make Jon understand.

Jon's thoughts were far away at that moment. With his spray-sprinkled face turned to the sun, and his eyes half-closed, it was as if he were caught in another age. He was a Viking at the tiller of his longboat; he was Captain Cook approaching an unknown Pacific Island; he was Columbus seeing the New World for the first time; he was. . . .

"Jon! Hard to starboard, else you'll have us on the rocks!"

His father's voice brought him back to the present with a bang, and he whipped the tiller around. "Sorry, Dad," he mumbled, "I was dreaming."

"Let's anchor in that inlet," said his father, having a quick look around. "It's shallow enough to wade ashore."

Deftly he guided the *Bonny Prince* into the inlet, and

dropped anchor within easy distance of the shore. Jon jumped out, causing a tremendous splash, and was quickly followed by his father and Joanna.

The rocks by the shore formed deep pools which hid many sea creatures. "Hey! Look at this crab," shouted Jon. "Ouch! the beast nipped me."

His father laughed. "Serves you right, Jon. You'd bite if someone held you up by one leg."

"Look at that fat fish," said Joanna. "Must have got trapped there when the tide went out."

Mr. Mackenzie leaned over the pool, and with a quick movement of his hand flipped the fish back into the sea.

Jon started to climb over the rocks. "Come on, let's explore this cave," he called presently.

The cave was high and narrow, but not very deep, and as the tide was low, they were able to wade quite easily into the entrance. The sounds echoed strangely inside the cave, and Joanna gave a frightened yelp as a small seabird suddenly flew out and banged her on the head.

"Can you see anything, Dad?" called Jon to his father, who was some yards ahead.

"It's too dark, really," said Mr. Mackenzie. "Could do with a flashlight. Doesn't go in very far."

"Look! There's a big ring embedded in the rock just here. What would you use that for?" Joanna was pointing to a large rock a little way in from the cave entrance.

"Fishing, maybe," Jon hazarded.

"I doubt it," said his father. "There's only room for one boat to tie up."

"Smugglers?" suggested Jo.

"That's more like it," said her father. "Plenty of that went on in the last century. The cave might have been deeper then. It looks as though there may have been a rock fall which has blocked the way."

Their eyes were becoming more accustomed to the dim light. They examined the rock face closely, but there was no sign of any way through it.

"Let's get back to the boat and sail on a bit further," said Jon, in a disgruntled tone. "There's nothing more here of any interest."

"All right," agreed Mr. Mackenzie. "We want to see as much as possible of the coast."

They retraced their steps to the cave entrance, where Joanna gave an exclamation of dismay. "Dad! The boat's sailing away!"

The others dashed to her side, and sure enough, there, prancing upon the waves, her bow pointed towards America, was the *Bonny Prince*.

"She must have dragged her anchor," said Jon, despondently. "What on earth are we going to do now?"

His father looked around. "There's only one way out, and that's up." He pointed to the towering cliff face behind them.

"No thanks," said Joanna, shaking her head. "Not in these rope sandals, Dad."

"Then we shall just have to wait," said her father in a resigned voice. "Someone's bound to miss us sooner or later."

"Hope it isn't later," muttered Jon. "I'm beginning to feel hungry."

Joanna laughed. "You're always hungry, Jon. It's not long since lunch."

"But there's Loch Fyne haddock for supper to-night—Mrs. Sinclair told me so, and it's my favorite. I don't want to miss that."

"Well, I'm going down to the pool again. It's better than just sitting here waiting," said Joanna.

She ran off to the large rock pool near where they had landed. Jon and his father sat near the cave entrance, looking out over the water and watching the *Bonny Prince* get smaller and smaller. The silence, which had remained unbroken for some time, apart from the shrill cries of the whirling gulls, was suddenly shattered by a piercing scream.

Jon and his father jumped to their feet and raced down to the pool. Joanna was cowering behind a large outcrop, and as they reached her, a rock whistled down past Jon's head, causing him to jump for cover. It broke into a thousand pieces as it hit the ground.

"Take cover, Jon, it's a rock fall!" shouted Mr. Mac-kenzie, as he put a comforting arm around his daughter's shoulders.

She was shaking violently, and her face was white as she said, "No, Dad, it's not a rock fall. Someone's trying to kill me. I saw him quite distinctly as he threw the first rock down!"

5
Rescue—and the Second Clue

Mr. Mackenzie stared at his daughter in disbelief, but another well-aimed rock from the cliff top made him realize that she was telling the truth. A chip from the shattered rock hit his cheek, and a small stream of blood started to trickle down his face.

Joanna gave a cry of dismay, but her father soaked his handkerchief in the rock pool and held it firmly against the cut.

"It's nothing," he said, reassuringly. "What a rotten trick! What does he think he will gain?"

With a clatter of falling stones, Jon made a headlong dive across to join them, and his momentary appearance was hailed by an avalanche of rocks from their assailant.

"Whew! That was close," said Jon with a wry grin. "Looks as though practice makes perfect."

"What are we going to do, Dad?" asked Joanna, clutching her father's arm. "He's got us pinned down here, and we couldn't even stand up to wave if a boat did come by."

"There must be something we can do," her father

replied, putting his arm comfortingly around her shoulders.

"What about a prayer, Jo?" said Jon. "Surely now's a good time for one."

"Excellent idea," said Mr. Mackenzie, quite missing the sarcasm in Jon's voice which had brought a flush to his sister's cheeks. "Let's all pray together."

He and Joanna bent their heads, and Jon, looking slightly abashed, did likewise.

"Loving Father," said Mr. Mackenzie quietly, "Thou knowest the plight we are in, and we ask Thee most humbly to deliver us from our enemies, and show us the way to safety. Amen."

As he lifted his head, a further avalanche of rocks came down, and the three cowered low in their hiding place.

"Not much deliverance about that," muttered Jon.

"Don't be irreverent, my boy," said his father. "It is in the Lord's hands now, and He will help us in His own good time."

The time passed slowly as they crouched uncomfortably behind the rock. For the hundredth time Jo looked towards the sea. "There's a boat coming," she said, excitedly.

Jon and his father turned cautiously to look. Sure enough, a small launch was chugging around the headland into the bay, and was towing behind it their sailing boat, the *Bonny Prince*.

"How can we signal?" asked Jon, anxiously.

Joanna had a sudden idea. "Pull off your shirt and wave it, Jon. They're bound to see that."

"Good idea," said her brother, whipping the T-shirt

over his head and waving it from side to side. A sudden shower of rocks indicated that the maneuver had been seen. But the silence that followed led them to believe that their attacker had taken to his heels.

"Seems like he's given up," observed Joanna, thankfully.

Mr. Mackenzie cautiously raised his head, but nothing happened. He looked all around.

"He could be seen by anyone on that boat, and possibly recognized. Probably thought he'd clear off while the going was good."

The launch chugged steadily nearer, and suddenly Joanna gave a shout. "It's Jamie! However did he know where to look for us?"

They all ran into the water as the launch cut its engine and drifted into the bay, the *Bonny Prince* gently losing way behind her. Throwing the rope to Mr. Mackenzie, Jamie jumped ashore.

"Oh, Jamie!" Joanna cried. "Are we glad to see you—we thought we might have to stay here all night."

"What happened to your boat?" asked Jamie.

"It drifted away—possibly by accident," said Mr. Mackenzie. "But it was no accident that someone has been hurling rocks at us from the top of the cliff. Trying to scare us off, I suppose."

"That's who I saw then," said Jamie. "As I rounded the headland, I could see a figure on the cliff top, but at first I thought it was one of you. Then it disappeared."

"Yes, he took himself off as soon as your boat came in sight," said Mr. Mackenzie. "He'll cut across the island to safety before we can set up any pursuit."

"This inlet is not very far from the house, you know," Jamie pointed out. "In fact, that is all 'San Salvador' property."

"Come on, then," said Mr. Mackenzie, "let's get home. Can you tow the sailing boat, Jamie? It'll be quicker than sailing her now that the wind's easing."

Jon opted to go in the *Bonny Prince* to steer her, and soon they were well out into the bay, the launch chugging gently along in the now placid water, the late afternoon sun casting a rosy glow over both boats.

Joanna looked at Jamie as he stood at the wheel, his blue eyes slightly crinkled as he stared ahead at the rocky coastline, a breeze rippling his thick, black hair. How wonderful that he had come along just when he was needed.

She sat up with a start. "Jamie! How did you know where to look for us? We didn't see you at lunch to tell you we were taking *Bonny Prince* out."

Her father looked around with interest.

Jamie wrinkled his forehead with a frown. "I'd been a bit on edge all day, worrying about Mother, and the strange happenings here since Mr. Hamish died. I'd worked near the house most of the time, and then, when I went in for a cup of tea, Mother told me you'd taken the *Bonny Prince* out. As I sat there, it suddenly occurred to me what a wonderful opportunity it would be for someone to put you all in danger by tampering with the boat. Once the thought was there, I couldn't rest until I'd investigated. I took the western passage, the way you came in from the East on the *Lochaber*. Then, as I was rounding Storm Point, I saw a small boat in the distance heading out to sea. I turned the launch, and on finding it was the *Bonny Prince*, I took her in tow. By the way, I meant to tell you before, the anchor chain had been almost sawn through, which is why she took off on her own.''

"So someone did have another try at us," said Mr. Mackenzie. "I suppose the man on the headland was there to check what happened."

"Probably," said Jamie, grimly.

"Oh well, we're safe now," said Mr. Mackenzie, giving Joanna a hug. "We knew that Jesus wouldn't let us down, didn't we, Jo?"

Joanna smiled happily at her father, and they continued their journey in silence, all three absorbed in their own thoughts.

* * * * * * *

Mrs. Mackenzie paled visibly when the adventure was recounted to her during the evening meal. "Things are really getting out of hand, Andrew," she said. "Can't the police do anything to help?"

"Well," said her husband, "Inspector Reid has been most understanding, but still seems to think that it's only a practical joke. Probably by someone who had a grudge against Uncle Hamish."

"But surely this latest outrage puts it beyond a mere practical joke," Mrs. Mackenzie insisted.

"Yes, it does that," her husband agreed, "but of course, the Inspector doesn't know anything about that yet. I'll give him a call after supper."

"I noticed you talking to Alistair MacBride before lunch, Andrew. Does he think it's all imagination?"

"Well, he did drop a few hints about not taking it too

seriously. Apparently he's met this fellow Gonzales in the village, and thinks he's pretty harmless, even if he does look like a scoundrel."

"I should think today's events will change his tune," said Mrs. Mackenzie rather tartly.

"Well, Mom, we don't exactly know that it was Gonzales who attacked us," Joanna pointed out. "I could see a figure on the cliff top, but I couldn't say who it was."

"Please be doubly careful now," her mother pleaded. "It seems to me we're all in danger, but you two particularly."

"We'll take care," said Joanna, planting a swift affectionate kiss on her mother's cheek. "I'm off to my room now. Coming, Jon?"

Jon nodded, and they went upstairs together.

* * * * * * *

Jon followed his sister into her room and flung himself down on a chair.

"We're getting nowhere fast, aren't we?" he said. "Seems to me the other side hold all the cards."

"Do they?" said Joanna, a slight smile twitching the corners of her lips. "I wonder."

"And just what do you mean by that cryptic remark?" asked Jon, glaring across at her as she searched through the bookcase.

"Take a look at this, Jon, and get those brain cells of yours working. I found it after we came in off the boat, so I didn't have time to show you before."

She handed Jon the copy of *Great Armada* by J. R. Hale, taken from the library.

"Don't tell me Great-Uncle Hamish has marked an

41

X on the map or something ridiculously simple like that," said Jon.

"No, it's nothing simple," his sister replied, "but it's definitely a clue. So we must get our thinking caps on. Look inside the back cover at the fly leaf."

Jon did so, and found that the last blank page in the book had been most ingeniously glued to the back cover to form a small pocket. Inside was a small slip of very thin paper. He unfolded it carefully, and found it contained several lists of numbers.

1598	1608	1603	1590	1614	1606	1612	1599
1603	1595	1598	1599	1606	1599	1603	1600
1595	1606	1598	1612	1599	1600	1601	1614
1612	1590	1599	1595	1614	1614	1602	1602
1593	1595	1608	1612	1591	1613	1614	1595
1609	1612	1603	1593	1599	1599	1613	1607
1600	1599	1608	1597	1608	1590	1603	1603
1598	1594	1603	1595	1614	1599	1592	1613
1609	1602	1608	1613	1593	1608	1606	1602

Jon stared at it for a moment, then threw it down on the table in disgust. "A clue, you say? You must be joking. Looks like a lot of amateur mathematics to me."

"Of course it's a clue," said Joanna, crossly. "Oh, don't be such a misery, Jon. Can't you see that it's a coded message? All we've got to do is break the code and it will probably tell us where the treasure is hidden."

"All we've got to do is break the code," mimicked Jon. "And that might take twenty years." He picked up the paper again and stared at it. "It looks as though you might be right," he conceded at last. "Get some paper and pencils, and we'll have a try."

The twins sat down at the small table with the list of numbers between them.

"How do we start?" asked Joanna.

"I don't really know," said Jon, tapping his pencil on the table. "Let's divide them into pairs and see what happens. After all, the alphabet only goes up to twenty-six, so there can't be four figure numbers. You take the top line and I'll take the second and we'll see how we get on."

Joanna started to break the first row down into pairs:

15 98 16 08 16 03 15 90

"That's not going to be any good, Jon," she said after a moment or two. "There's no number to correspond with 98 in the alphabet, and the numbers are alternately high and low doing it that way. No, I think each set of four numbers represents one letter."

"But how can they?" her brother protested. "The numbers are too high."

"Yes, but if we could find the keyword or number. . . ."

"Oh yes, if. . . ." Jon said bitterly. "Life's too full of 'ifs' at the moment if you ask me."

He bent over the paper again and wrote down all the groups of numbers. "I'll take this to bed with me and sleep on it," he said to his sister, getting to his feet. "I'm getting sleepy—aren't you?"

"A little," Joanna confessed. "Oughtn't we to tell Dad about our discovery? He may know how to crack the code."

"Good idea—we'll tell him tomorrow and get his

brain working on it. See you in the morning, Jo." He opened the door and started to leave.

"Oh, Jon," his sister called, "don't leave that code lying around, will you? If Gonzales suspects that we've found something, he may search our rooms, and if we lose the code we've had it—it's our only clue."

"I'll be careful, Jo. Goodnight," and he went out.

Joanna looked thoughtfully at the coded message, then sat down at the table and began quietly copying the numbers on to a similar sized piece of paper. This she inserted in the pocket at the back of *Great Armada* and replaced the book on the shelf. The original paper she folded carefully and placed within the pages of her Bible.

As she moved across to pull the curtains, the moon moved from behind a cloud, clearly outlining the lawn and the trees beyond. A shadow flitted quickly from tree to tree, pausing now and again to peer around before moving on. Joanna watched, and saw the figure disappear towards the woods. She looked at her watch—it was half past eleven.

Grabbing a jacket from the chair, she tiptoed across the hall to Jon's bedroom and tapped on the door— their secret signal—three short, two long, two short. The door opened quickly and she slipped inside.

"Get your coat quick, Jon," she whispered. "I've just seen someone hurrying through the trees towards the woods. I think they must be making their way to the Spanish Oak. They probably have a rendezvous for midnight. We must try and follow him."

Jon needed no second bidding. He grabbed his coat and flashlight, and pushed Joanna out through the

44

door, closing it quietly behind him. They tiptoed downstairs, avoiding the step that creaked, and reaching the side door, slipped the bolts and hurried out.

There was a bite in the air and the grass felt damp under their feet, but everything was very still. Reaching the line of trees, Jon paused.

"Which way?" he whispered.

"Towards the woods. Jamie said the Spanish Oak was there."

"Keep your eyes and ears alert," whispered her brother. "We don't want to get caught."

They went on as quietly as possible, flitting from one tree to another, and listening for some indication as to where their quarry might be. Suddenly Jon stopped so abruptly that Joanna, who had been watching where she put her feet, cannoned into him. He grabbed her arm and whispered, "Over there," pointing ahead through the gloom. Just at that moment, the moon appeared briefly from its cloud cover, and the twins could see the outline of a dark figure a short distance away, leaning against the trunk of a large tree. They froze like statues as the figure appeared to look their way. Then they heard a low, three-note whistle, and the figure turned abruptly.

A second person emerged through the trees and joined him under the Spanish Oak. They turned their backs and stood with heads bent, conversing together. Jon touched his sister's arm and pointed. Ahead and a little to their left was a thick holly bush, and behind it a fallen tree. Quickly and quietly the twins tiptoed across until they were hidden behind it, and only a few feet away from the two men.

"We've come to a dead end," said one voice. "Today I had them really frightened over in Toward Bay, but Sinclair turned up in the launch and I had to scarper."

"Never mind," said the other man, testily. "I'm sure the Mackenzie children have found something, and we must learn what it is. It can't have been around at the cove; it must have been in the house. That's where you come in, Gonzales; you must find it, by fair means or foul."

"The Mackenzies searched the secret room next morning, and only found a letter that told them nothing. Still, I'll have another scout around."

"Perhaps it's time for another warning."

"I'll see to it tomorrow, Miguel. If we could scare them away, our task would be much simpler—we'd only have the Sinclairs to deal with."

An owl suddenly hooted from a branch just above their heads, and Gonzales muttered a curse.

"I must go now," said Miguel. "Tomorrow night, same time and place. And have something to report," and he melted away into the darkness.

Gonzales muttered something and strode away through the trees, passing close to where the twins were hiding.

"I'll tell you something," said Jon in a low tone, as soon as Gonzales had disappeared, "that Gonzales is no more a Spaniard than I am. And as for that other man, I'm sure I've heard his voice somewhere. What did you think?"

He turned around and found that he was alone.

Joanna had disappeared!

6

The Twins Are Captured

Jon looked around in dismay. "Jo!" he called urgently. "Joanna! Where are you?"

"Here! Here I am, Jon. Give me some help, quick!"

The voice came almost from beneath his feet, and Jon shone his flashlight downwards. In front of him yawned a great hole, and he could see Joanna's head peering out of it.

"Jo! Are you all right?"

"I think so. I seem to have gone straight down a hole, and I'm standing on a ledge of some sort. Do you think you can pull me up?" She gingerly reached her hand out towards him.

Jon took a grasp of it firmly, and hitched his other arm around the trunk of the nearest tree, bracing his feet against the roots.

"Right you are then, Jo. Up we come."

He gave a big heave, and gradually Jo emerged from the hole, covered with dirt and twigs. Jon helped her to a seat on the fallen tree, then taking the flashlight, he played the beam carefully down the hole.

"Jo!" he said, excitedly. "It looks like—" he moved the beam from side to side. "Yes, it looks like a stone staircase. We must come back in daylight and investigate. Are you all right to walk now?"

"Yes, I'm all right. Just wondered where I was off to, that's all."

"Come on, then, let's go home and get some sleep—and we won't tell anyone about this until we've had a look ourselves."

* * * * * * *

As breakfast finished the next morning, Mr. Mackenzie looked across at the twins. "And what have you two got lined up for this morning?"

"Well, we thought we'd go and have a look around the woods again—just in case we've missed any clues," said Jon. "Also, Dad, we've made a discovery—Jo will tell you about it."

Mr. and Mrs. Mackenzie looked expectantly at their daughter.

"You remember that letter you found from Great-Uncle Hamish? At the end of it, he recommended a book for you to read. Well, I found the book in the library and looked at it. Inside a little pocket in the back cover, I found a sheet of paper covered with numbers."

"A code message!" said her father, excitedly. "Where is it now?"

"Jon and I tried the code last night, but we couldn't make any headway with it. We thought perhaps you and Mom might have a try." She handed him a slip of paper.

Mr. Mackenzie studied the paper carefully. "Hm! We'll have a go at this, and I promise I'll guard it with my life."

The twins laughed and went out into the garden, where Jon picked up a large knapsack.

"Help! What do you have there?" asked Joanna.

"Just a few things we might need. Flashlights, a rope, a couple of knives, a digging tool. Oh! and some food, of course."

"Of course," said his sister, with a twinkle in her eye. And they set off towards the woods.

They found the Spanish Oak quite easily as daylight revealed a well-trodden path leading directly towards it. A few seconds later, they were at the hole. Jon found the digging tool and they quickly cleared the area around the opening.

"Looks as though there might have been a trapdoor here at one time," said Jon, peering down the hole, "but it's cracked with age—your weight just about finished it off."

"What do you mean—my weight?" asked Joanna, indignantly. "I'm not as heavy as all that."

"I know," Jon said grinning. "You just happened to stand on the crack, I expect. Come on, I'm going down."

Repacking the knapsack, and taking a flashlight in his hand, he made his way down the narrow flight of steps with Joanna close behind. There was a dank, musty smell from the tunnel, which branched off in opposite directions at the foot of the steps.

"Which way shall we try?" Joanna whispered.

Jon shone the flashlight all around while they took their bearings. The tunnel was high enough for them to stand, and appeared to have been cut out of solid rock. They could hear a distant drip, drip, drip as water

49

seeped through from the surface, but otherwise there was no sound.

"Let's try the left tunnel first," said Jon. "That should lead back to the house. Then we'll come back and try the other one."

He led the way slowly, shining the light on either side as he went. Joanna let out a terrified squeak as a small furry creature ran over her foot and disappeared into the darkness. A few more minutes brought them to another flight of stone steps with an oak door at the top. Jon looked at his sister and raised his eyebrows. She nodded, and he quietly mounted the steps and took hold of the door knob. It turned easily.

"This is well oiled," he commented, quietly, "so someone must use if pretty often."

Gently he pushed the door open, and they found themselves in a dusty passageway with thick walls on either side. Jon shone his flashlight around. "It's like a little room," he said, "but there's no other way out. I wonder what it was used for?"

"There must be a way in from the house," Joanna said, "else there's no point in it. Shine your flashlight along this opposite wall."

Jon did as she suggested, and after a few moments, the beam settled on a small knob fastened to some primitive mechanism. Jon quickly moved the knob, and a section of the wall slid open. Going through, they found that a whole panel of bookshelves on one wall of the library had moved behind the one next to it, leaving an opening wide enough for one person to pass through.

"I wonder how it works from this side," said Joanna.

"Close the panel, Jon, and I'll see if I can find the catch."

Jon went inside and operated the knob. Joanna watched and easily found the particular motif on the decorated panelling which would open it again. A few seconds later she was inside with Jon, and the panel closed again.

"I reckon this is how Gonzales got into the house," Jon said. "I don't think he came in through the window at all, but I believe he went out that way so that we wouldn't know about this secret tunnel."

Joanna nodded, then grabbed his arm as they heard voices from the library. It was their parents.

"Try not to worry, Myra," Mr. Mackenzie was saying. "We've put the matter in God's hands, and He will take care of it for us. We must trust Him."

"I do," replied his wife. "It's only that. . . ."

"I know. Jon and Joanna. But we've placed them in God's care too, and we *know* He will not fail us. Now, about this code. After dinner we'll settle down and have a try at it, Myra," their father continued. "I'd like to prove to the twins that I'm not such a fuddy-duddy as they seem to think."

Their voices were quite sharp and clear, and Jon soon realized why. One small panel was perforated with tiny holes, invisible from the other side, but enough to allow the sound to penetrate.

"So that's how they learned Great-Uncle Hamish's secret," muttered Jon. "Come on, let's explore the other end of the tunnel."

Quickly closing the outer door, they carefully retraced their steps. On reaching their starting point, they realized that Jon's idea had been correct, for a large flagstone lay broken in the tunnel near the steps.

"You were fortunate to land on your feet, Jo," her brother said. "Another inch and you'd have fallen right to the bottom."

"My guardian angel must have been looking after me," Joanna said, but there was no reply from her brother.

Slowly they moved along the dank, evil-smelling tunnel.

"Phew!" said Jon, "this smell is getting worse. Must be quite near the sea I should think."

They stopped and listened, but heard nothing apart from the steady drip of water. A little later the tunnel opened out into a wide cave, with one or two dark openings along the far side, which were probably more tunnels.

"It's like a rabbit warren down here," Jon said, quietly.

Further exploration showed that the cave had recently been inhabited, or more probably still was. There was a rough table with the remains of a meal on it, a couple of empty bottles, one holding the stump of a candle, and a wooden box for a seat. In the corner was an old trestle bed with a sleeping bag flung carelessly on top, a large knapsack, and an old ship's lantern.

"Gonzales' hide-out!" breathed Joanna.

"Yes," said Jon. "I wonder where he is now."

Scarcely had he spoken, when there was an ominous click behind them. The twins whipped around, ready to run, but they were too late. Outlined in the tunnel entrance was the menacing figure of Gonzales, holding a knife in his right hand.

"So," he muttered, "you decided to ignore my warnings. You will be sorry, my leetle friends, you will be verree sorry."

He moved slowly towards them, and the twins cowered back against the wall.

"You won't gain anything by killing us," said Jon bravely. "My father will never give in. And you can cut out that phoney accent, too—we know you're not a Spaniard."

A snarl came from Gonzales. "So, you are getting too clever. Suppose I send your father one of your sister's curls, and maybe perhaps a finger! What then?" His teeth bared in a menacing grin. "Ah yes, your father will give me what I want. Never fear."

Joanna gave a whimper of fear and moved closer to her brother, who put his arm protectingly around her shoulders, displaying a courage he was far from feeling.

"What—what are you going to do with us?"

"For the moment I'll lock you up somewhere safe, and then I will see Miguel." He carefully lit the candle on the table, its flickering flame making grotesque shadows on the walls.

"Who is Miguel?"

"He is my friend—he is the brains and I am the brawn, you might say," Gonzales answered silkily, rubbing his thumb gently up and down the sharp blade of the knife. "He will know how to make the best use of you."

He moved swiftly towards them, indicating with the

knife that he wished them to enter the small side tunnel. "Here you will be safe," he said, "that is, unless you can chew your way through solid rock."

Inside, the tunnel was even wetter and smellier than the previous one. Water ran down the walls, making large puddles on the damp, sandy floor. Set high in the rock wall was a row of large iron rings. Gonzales motioned the twins towards them.

"Face the wall," he growled at Joanna, poking the knife in her ribs.

When she did so, trembling with fear, Gonzales quickly slipped the knife between his teeth, and taking some rope, tied Jon's wrists tightly to the rings above his head. Then he did the same to Joanna.

"There, that should keep you quiet for a while," he said, gazing in admiration at his handiwork. The twins were tied, face to the wall, with arms above their heads. The rings were set so high that they were almost standing on tiptoe. "Even if you do escape, this tunnel leads only to the sea. I go to find Miguel."

And he left them, stopping at the tunnel entrance to lower a metal grille, sealing off what little light there had been.

"Oh, Jon," moaned Joanna. "Whatever can we do? I've got pins and needles already, and my arms feel as if they're being pulled out of their sockets. Is there any hope?"

"I slipped my jackknife into my shirt pocket; perhaps if I wiggle around I can reach it with my mouth."

"What good will that do?" asked Joanna. "You'll never be able to open it, and even if you could, how would you reach the ropes to cut them?"

Jon groaned. "You're right, of course. It would be a wasted effort."

The time passed very slowly. When their eyes became fully accustomed to the gloom, Joanna could see Jon was struggling with his ropes, but not accomplishing anything. He paused and glanced at the luminous dial on his watch.

"Half past one," he said. "There goes that gorgeous dinner Mrs. Sinclair had prepared for us. Mom and Dad will be worried stiff. If only we'd stopped to tell them about the tunnel."

But it was too late for wishing that.

7

The Search
and the Escape

Back at "San Salvador," their father was pacing up and down the library while his wife sat quietly in an armchair watching him, her face pale and strained.

"Something must have happened to them," Mr. Mackenzie said at last. "Nothing would make Jon miss his dinner—nothing. I'm sure something's happened."

"What are you going to do?" asked Myra, anxiously. "We don't really know where to start looking. What about the police?"

"I don't know that they've been missing long enough for the police to worry—they seem to think it's all a practical joke anyway. There is only one thing we can do to help. Let us pray together for their safety, Myra. We know that Jesus will take care of them."

They knelt together in silent prayer, knowing that with Jesus all things are possible, and that He will never leave us to carry our burdens alone.

Mr. Mackenzie rose from his knees wearily. "I'll call Jamie and ask him to scout around first," he said.

Just as he was about to press the bell, the door burst

open and a man rushed into the room. It was Alistair MacBride.

"Andrew! Myra!" he gasped, breathlessly. "Dreadful news. The twins have been kidnapped!"

Mr. and Mrs. Mackenzie stared at him in horror. Myra rose slowly to her feet as if in a dream, her eyes a vivid blue against the whiteness of her face.

"How—how do you know?" she asked.

Alistair MacBride held out a piece of paper. "I was coming over to take you all for a drive around the island, and a stone was thrown into the carriage with this note wrapped around it."

The note was brief and to the point:

I HAVE THE TWINS. I WILL EXCHANGE THEM FOR THE SECRET OF THE TREASURE. AWAIT FURTHER INSTRUCTIONS.

Mr. Mackenzie dashed to the phone and began to dial. Alistair MacBride took the receiver from his hand and clamped it down again.

"Is that wise, Andrew? Do you want to endanger the lives of your children even more?" he asked quietly.

Mr. Mackenzie stared blankly at him, then sat down with his head in his hands.

"But what are we to do?" asked Myra. "We can't just sit here and wait."

"A search party," said her husband, suddenly. "We must get up a search party. See if Jamie's in to lunch."

Myra ran quickly out and returned a few seconds later followed by Jamie, who was munching a sandwich.

"How many men can you raise for a search party to look for the twins?" Mr. Mackenzie asked, his brow puckering anxiously. "We've found a note saying they've been kidnapped, and they haven't been back for lunch."

"There are three working on the harvest," said Jamie, swallowing hastily, "and Frazer's over mending the tractor. He'll help. Where do we start?"

"That's the trouble," said Mr. Mackenzie, rubbing his fingers through his hair, "we don't really know. The children said they were going to the woods, so I'd suggest you start there, and then spread along the cliffs. If you find nothing, we must extend the search to the rest of the island—it isn't very large, after all."

"But where could they hide them?" asked Myra. "The villagers all know us—they would hardly be a party to such a dreadful thing. Are there any old cottages or huts where they could be?"

"Aye. There are several shepherds' huts up on the hillside. I'll send a man to sound them out first." Jamie paused, his firm features set in a worried frown. "The trouble is—" he looked at his employers, "there are quite a number of tunnels through these cliffs, used by smugglers in days gone by. We'll have a rare time looking for the twins if they've been taken there."

"Let's not look on the black side," said Mr. Mackenzie, hastily. "Off you go, Jamie—MacBride and I will join you in a little while."

"Aye," agreed Alistair. "I have the carriage we can use to check whether they've been seen elsewhere on the island."

Jamie hurried to the door, then paused and turned

back. "Mr. Mackenzie," he said, deferentially, "I ken ye've no told the police. Why? Surely we could do with some help?"

Mr. Mackenzie looked haggard. "Yes, we could that. But Mr. MacBride feels we may be endangering the lives of the children by calling in the police. I—I don't know—but I can't afford to take the risk. Make a start, Jamie, there's a good chap."

Jamie turned his eyes upon Alistair MacBride with a long, penetrating stare, then went out without another word.

* * * * * * *

Back in the cave, Jon and Joanna were desperately trying to find a firm foothold in the rock to take the weight off their tired wrists.

Suddenly there was a grating noise in the doorway. The grille lifted and Gonzales came in.

"I came back to see if you were still 'ere," the Spaniard said, grinning.

"How long are you going to keep us here?" asked Joanna, anxiously.

"Until the senor 'ands over the secret of the treasure."

"But he hasn't got it," cried Joanna.

"But you 'ave the clue—we know that, and if 'e 'ands it over, then 'e will get you back alive."

"And—if he doesn't?" asked Jon.

Gonzales gave a dry, cackling laugh. "That weel give you something to think about, won't it, young master?"

"All we've found is the coded message in the back

of a book called *The Great Armada*," Joanna burst out, in spite of a warning look from her brother. "There's nothing else, and we haven't been able to crack the code, so what *can* my father tell you?" Her voice rose hysterically on the last word, and she was close to tears.

Gonzales cackled again. "Do you expect me to believe that 'amish Mackenzie put the treasure secret in code, told you where to find eet, then forgot to give you the key! No, eet ees not possible. Tonight your father will tell us, you'll see. Now I must go."

Giving another loud cackle, Gonzales picked up the lantern and left them in the dark, carefully closing the grille behind him.

"Now what?" whispered Joanna. "If Dad and Mom know we've been kidnapped, they're not likely to sit at home all afternoon trying to crack that code."

"No," agreed her brother, "they'll be out searching, may even have called the police in to help. But we're not going to wait here to be rescued."

"What do you mean?" asked Joanna.

"Gonzales was in such a hurry that he didn't notice that this right-hand ring is loose in the rock," said Jon. "I had a good look when the lantern was here, and if I wiggle it around long enough, perhaps I can pull it out."

The minutes ticked by slowly.

As Jon jerked the ring backwards and forwards, the perspiration poured down his face, and his breath came in loud, choking gasps. Then he heard Jo's voice speaking very softly and earnestly:

"Dear Jesus, help Jon now. Even if he doesn't believe

60

he needs Your help. You told us once to ask for what we wanted, and if we had faith our request would be granted. I know, Lord, that You can help us; You are our only hope, and I trust You, dear Jesus, to keep your promise. Amen."

Jon paused to rest. Certainly they needed help now more than ever. Joanna was quite right to pray; it couldn't do any harm, and it might—it just might, he conceded—do some real good.

"Can you sing something, Jo?" he said. "Just in case Gonzales is around—I don't want him to get suspicious."

Jo thought, and then, her voice starting feebly but growing in strength, she sang:

"Walk Thou with me, nor let my footsteps stray,
Apart from Thee, throughout life's threatening
  way,
Be Thou my Guide, the path I cannot see,
Close to Thy side, Lord, let me walk with Thee.

Dear Savior, let me trust my hand in Thine,
And let me know Thy steps are guiding mine,
Life's changing way is oft-times dark to me,
I fear no ill if I may walk with Thee."

Jon resumed his efforts, and some minutes later the ring pulled away from the wall with a loud clang, and a cloud of dust nearly choked them.

Jon was swinging backwards and forwards, with all his weight suspended on one arm. Frantically he scrabbled with his feet, trying to find a foothold. Making a supreme effort, he managed to lever himself up until his

61

finger tips touched the hole in the rock face, and he was able to take the weight off his other arm.

"Phew!" he said. "I thought I'd had it then. My wrist was nearly pulled out of its socket."

"How can you get your other arm undone?" asked Joanna.

"Now I've got a good foothold, I'm going to try and grab the other ring with my free hand. Then I might be able to get the rope untied."

Gripping the rock wall as firmly as he could with his feet, he suddenly let go with his right hand and made a frantic grab at the ring to which his left hand was tied, tearing his finger nails on the rock, but managing to hold on to his own wrist as his body swung back.

"Made it," he muttered, and started to work on the rope. It was not easy as the weight of his body was pulling the rope taut, but by moving his feet a little and pressing hard against the rock face with his body, he found he could manage to release the rope. The fingers of his left hand were numb, and as the last knot came undone, the rope tore through the ring and Jon crashed to the ground.

"Jon!" Joanna screamed, peering through the gloom. "Are you all right?"

There was a groan from the floor and Jon sat up, rubbing his head ruefully. "It's a good thing I've got a hard head," he said. "I forgot about the rope pulling through like that."

It took only a few moments to release the ring from his right wrist and to cut his sister's ropes. Then Jon sank exhausted to the floor, his head between his knees.

Joanna slipped her arm around his shoulders and gave him a hug.

"Rest for a while, Jon. At least we're free of those beastly ropes—thanks to you."

Jon did not answer. His body felt drained of energy and he just sat there, breathing deeply until he felt the blood circulating freely through his tortured wrists, and his strength began to return.

After a while he lifted his head, stretched himself and turned to his sister.

"We must get out, Jo. We've no idea when Gonzales may come back, and I don't want to be here when that happens. Is the outside room empty?"

Joanna crept to the grille and listened. "Can't hear anyone moving about," she said.

"Open up then," said Jon, getting slowly to his feet.

Joanna reached through the gap at the side and tugged at the lever which operated the grille, but nothing happened.

"It's no good, Jon," she said at last. "Gonzales must have locked the mechanism."

"Then there's nothing for it but the tunnel," said Jon, rather despondently. "Did he leave us our knapsack?" He looked around him, but the cave floor was bare. "Come on then, Jo. Follow me closely and if I say stop, stop quickly. We don't know what we're likely to find, and we'll have to feel our way along very carefully."

And they set off, slowly and cautiously, into the dark unknown ahead.

* * * * * * *

Meanwhile, the search for the twins had been going

on methodically, but with no success. No trace of them had been found. Mrs. Mackenzie, assisted by Mrs. Sinclair, had searched the house and its immediate grounds, and had been instructed to stay near the telephone. The men had divided up into groups. One man had gone to search the shepherds' huts on the hill; Jamie and Frazer had searched the woods, cliffs, and beach; two men had been detailed to search the woods; and Mr. Mackenzie and Alistair MacBride were in the carriage scouring the outlying country-side. Finally, Jamie and his men straggled back, weary and despondent, to report that their search had brought no results.

"Come into the kitchen," said Mrs. Sinclair. "I've hot tea waiting for you and some sandwiches."

The men followed her out, and started in hungrily on the food she had prepared.

Jamie hastily swallowed a cup of scalding tea and turned to his mother. "I'm away, out in the boat. Frazer will come with me. We'll examine the cliffs as close in as we can get, and see if we can spot anything. Tell Mr. Mackenzie when he gets back."

"Ye'll tak care, Jamie," said his mother, anxiously. "Those rocks are awful dangerous."

"Aye, Mother. We'll take care." Jamie planted a swift kiss on her cheek, signaled to Frazer, and, grabbing a couple of sandwiches, was gone.

* * * * * * *

The twins edged their way slowly along the narrow, damp, twisting tunnel. Joanna tripped over a rock and fell full length into the wet, smelly mud, and Jon banged his elbow hard on a protruding ledge.

"Why haven't we come to daylight?" asked Joanna. "I didn't think we were far from the sea."

"I think this was probably an old underground river at one time; that's why it winds so much—it cut its way through the soft rock many years ago, but has now dried up."

"Not entirely," said Joanna, sarcastically, still trying to wipe the wet mud off herself.

"Be careful now," called Jon. "This is a tricky place as there's been a rockfall."

They clambered over the pile of boulders and, to their delight, saw a small circle of daylight ahead.

"Eureka!" shouted Jon, and hurried forward to find out where they were.

They found the narrow cave entrance was some twenty feet up a precipitous cliff face which seemed to fall sheer into the sea. They could not see up because of the rock overhang.

"If only we had a rope," wailed Joanna.

"If Gonzales had left us our knapsack, that piece of rope I put in might have been long enough," said her brother. "As it is, the only thing is to climb down. There looks to be plenty of hand and footholds."

"But will we be able to get away even if we do climb down the cliff?" asked Joanna.

"I don't know, but anything's better than staying here and waiting to be caught when Gonzales comes back."

Slowly and carefully he lowered himself over the edge of the cave mouth and, finding a firm foothold, prepared to start his climb down.

Suddenly Jo heard a grating noise, and saw to her

horror that the cave edge to which Jon was still holding was beginning to crack.

"Jon!" she screamed, "the rock's—"

But she was too late. With a rending noise the rock broke free, and Jon was sent hurtling into the sea below.

8
The Code Is Cracked

Jamie guided the launch along the rocky coastline with an expert hand. The sun was getting low on the horizon, and long shadows spread across the rippling surface of the sea.

"What do you hope to find?" Frazer asked, as he watched the cliffs, shading his eyes against the brightness of the sun's rays.

"I don't know," Jamie replied, grimly. "A boat perhaps, or some careless clue left behind. We've searched everywhere else, and to my mind the only place left will be the tunnels in the cliffs."

Frazer looked horrified. "But my dad used to say those tunnels stretch right through the island. It would take months to search them. I've only ever been in the few near the water's edge, and certainly never far inside—not out of daylight, that is."

"Well, if it comes to it, we'll have to search them—even if it takes the rest of our lives." Jamie's voice was stern, and his features set and hard.

"I'd not like to be in Gonzales' shoes if ye get your hands on him," Frazer remarked, glancing at the rigid countenance beside him.

"Nor the one who's giving the orders, either," Jamie replied.

"Ye think there's two of them then."

"I'm absolutely sure of it. Gonzales is no' the man to be doing this off his own bat. He's only the tool. But I'll find him, never fear. I'll find him."

Jamie steered the launch out into deeper water to clear the headland, his eyes never leaving the cliff face as he did so. The chug, chug, chug of the motor echoed eerily across the still water.

Suddenly Jamie stiffened, his knuckles showing white as he gripped the wheel.

"What was that?" he said.

Both men listened intently, their eyes glued to the cliffs. Frazer pointed to the far side of the bay. "Over there," he said briefly.

Jamie revved up the motor and the launch sped across the water. As the cliffs became clearer, his keen eyes picked out the figure of Joanna at the cave entrance halfway up the cliff face, calling and waving frantically.

"Can't see Jon anywhere," he remarked to Frazer. "Wonder what's happened to him."

"Can you hear what she's calling?"

They raced in closer, and Jamie cut the engine. "Where's Jon?" he shouted.

Joanna was frantic. "He fell—into the water. Oh, Jamie, please hurry and look. He must be there somewhere."

The two men quickly looked around, and there, partially hidden from view, they saw Jon. He was jammed up against a rock, his clawing fingers having hooked themselves into some thick seaweed. He had a nasty cut on his head, with blood slowly trickling down his face, and even as they spotted him, the fingers relaxed their grip, and he disappeared under the water.

Jamie whipped off his shoes and shirt, and dived overboard. With powerful strokes he soon reached the spot where Jon had gone down. A few seconds later he reappeared, holding the boy in his arms. Frazer held out the boathook to him and pulled them quickly to the side of the launch. Frazer lifted the boy from Jamie's arms, laid him in the bottom of the boat, and began pumping the water out of him. Jamie heaved himself up, and after a few minutes relieved Frazer. They worked in silence, turn and turn about; then there was a choking cough, a rasping intake of breath.

"Looks like he'll do now," said Frazer.

"Aye." Jamie stared at the boy, watching the first flush of color begin to spread over his cheeks. "But it was touch and go. We must get home fast and get Dr. Gordon."

"What about Miss Joanna? We canna leave her behind."

"No." Jamie stood and looked up at the anxious Joanna, who had been kneeling in the cave mouth watching the proceedings in the boat below.

"He'll do, Joanna, but we must get him back for Dr. Gordon to see him. Can you jump into the water? It's deep just here, you've no need to fear if you dive well out. I'll stand off a bit."

Suiting his actions to his words, Jamie started up the engine and stood the launch off a short way. He looked up at Joanna.

"Now!" he called.

Joanna was ready. She took off from the ledge in a well executed swallow dive into the deep water, and a few minutes later, was pulled, gasping and dripping, into the boat.

* * * * * * *

Jon's injuries proved to be slight, apart from the cut, but Dr. Gordon insisted on his remaining in bed the next day, just as a precaution. Jon was bored and irritable at having to stay in bed, until eventually Joanna got a little bit short with him.

"Oh Jon!" she said at last, "you've only got to stay there today—not for the rest of your life. Here, have another try at cracking this code."

"That's an idea," said Jon, showing some interest at last. "Throw over that pad and pencil, please."

"Has the headache gone?" Jo asked, as she passed them over.

"Yes, it's only a little sore now." He paused and looked at her thoughtfully. "You know, Jo, it's funny, but when I hit my head and went under, the only thing I could think of was what you'd said about believing in God and how I'd laughed at it. I was frightened, Jo, really frightened. I felt lost and I panicked."

"It's only natural, Jon. If Jamie hadn't arrived just when he did, you would have—"

"Died? Yes, probably. But in that moment of panic, Jo, I—I prayed. The first real prayer I've prayed in years. Oh, I know I did it in fear, but it was answered. Even though I denied Him, my prayer was still answered."

70

"Jesus loves you just the same, Jon, whether you deny Him or not."

"Yes," murmured Jon. "I really believe He does. You must help me, Jo—help me to get back to Him."

"The message of salvation is so simple, Jon. Just believe in Jesus, and accept His sacrifice on the Cross. He died to save us from our sins. He just wants you to surrender your life to Him, and He will guide you and watch over you. He also wants you to be an example to others so that they may be drawn to Him, too. Study the Bible each day, Jon. You'll find it a tremendous help."

The door opened and their mother came in carrying a tray with drinks and cookies.

"Hello there," she said with a smile. "Having fun? I thought you'd like some refreshments."

"Great!" said Jon. "I'm starving."

"Obviously well on the way to recovery," his mother said, winking at Joanna. "What are you doing?"

"Trying to crack the code. Has Dad tried it, or has he been too busy?"

"Well, we've both been trying, but without much success. It doesn't seem to fit into any nice simple pattern. Daddy seems to think there's a keyword or key number which we must find. We tried all the words we could think of but it was no good."

"What do you mean by a key number?" asked Joanna, with a puzzled frown.

"Daddy says that in some codes a key number is chosen which is known to agents. This number is added to each of the simple code numbers—just to complicate it, in fact." Mrs. Mackenzie picked up the paper with

71

the code message. "He suggested it might be a four figure number between 1,000 and 2,000, as there's no figure higher than that. If you can find the number, you'll probably be left with just a simple code." She looked at her watch. "Now, I must go and see if Mrs. Sinclair is coping with dinner. Dr. Gordon and Mr. MacBride are coming over."

She hurried out, and the twins bent to their task again.

"That key number idea sounds a possibility. Any suggestions?" asked Jon.

"What about the year Great-Uncle Hamish was born?" said Joanna.

"Do we know it?"

"No, but somebody must."

Jon studied the figures again. "No, it can't be that because he must have been born in eighteen hundred and something, and there's nothing higher than—" he searched down the list "—than 1614. And the lowest number is 1590. So logically. . . ."

Joanna shot off the bed in a sudden movement which caused Jon to drop his pencil in surprise.

"What on earth. . . ." he began.

She stared at him with shining eyes. "Jon—I think I've got it. What possible number could it be than the date of the Spanish Armada—1588? That was the book Great-Uncle Hamish put the code in. Quick, let's try it and see what we get."

Hastily the two grabbed pencil and paper and while Joanna subtracted 1588 from the original numbers, Jon wrote them down on a sheet of paper.

10	20	15	2	26	18	24	11
15	7	10	11	18	11	15	12
7	18	10	24	11	12	13	26
24	2	11	7	26	26	14	14
5	7	20	24	3	25	26	7
21	24	15	5	11	11	25	19
12	11	20	9	20	2	15	15
10	6	15	7	26	11	4	25
21	14	20	25	5	20	18	14

"That's much more like it," said Jon. "Now where's that chart we made yesterday?"

Rummaging through the papers on his side table, Jon soon found the two sheets of paper he was looking for—one bearing the letters of the alphabet, and the other the numbers 1 to 26.

"Let's take this top left-hand corner block of seven numbers and do them first. If it starts making sense, we can then apply that code to the whole message."

He carefully wrote out again the corner numbers:

10	20	15	2
15			
7			
24			

and then began moving the list of numbers along under the row of letters, first making A equal 2, then 3 and so on.

But Jo, who had been studying the new list of numbers intently, said suddenly: "Wait a minute, Jon, isn't E the most frequently used letter in the alphabet? The number 11 is used nine times in the code. Why not make E equal 11 and try that first?"

"Good idea," agreed Jon.

He immediately did as she suggested, moving the list of numbers along until E appeared above the number 11. Then he wrote down:

D   N   I   V
I
A
R

"That's it!" shrieked Joanna. "The 'down' letters —D I A R—diary!"

"Calm down a bit while I write it all out," said Jon, trying to conceal his own excitement. It took only a few minutes to complete the whole message.

D	N	I	V	T	L	R	E
I	A	D	E	L	E	I	F
A	L	D	R	E	F	G	T
R	V	E	A	T	T	H	H
Y	A	N	R	W	S	T	A
O	R	I	Y	E	E	S	M
F	E	N	C	N	V	I	I
D	Z	I	A	T	E	X	S
O	H	N	S	Y	N	L	H

Jon read it aloud, slowly. "Diary of Don Alvarez hidden in Inverary Castle twenty left seven right six left. Hamish. We've done it, Jo, we've done it."

"Yes, but what does it mean—'hidden in Inverary Castle'? That's miles away from here."

"We must ask Dad—he might have some suggestions," said Jon.

There was a brisk knock on the door and Dr. Gordon came in.

"Well, young man," he said, with a broad smile, "I hear you're fed up with confinement in bed. How about coming down to join us for dinner?"

"Great!" said Jon. "I'm tired of sitting here playing these stupid pencil and paper games. Besides, I'm starving!"

"You always are," said his sister, as she went out with Dr. Gordon.

* * * * * * *

Dinner that evening was quite a relaxed affair. For the time being, the burden of fear seemed to have been lifted from the Mackenzie family, and everyone was in a light-hearted mood. Mrs. Sinclair had excelled herself, and prepared all Jon's favorite dishes, to which he did full justice.

"At least your appetite is not impaired," commented his father, drily.

"Well," said Jon, giving the matter weighty consideration. "I may be a little off my food, but I shall be back to normal tomorrow."

He looked surprised at the roar of laughter from the others.

"Tell me, Jon," said Mr. MacBride, stroking his moustache, "how did you get into that cave in the first place? You surely didn't climb down from the cliff top?"

"Oh no," said Jon. "It was purely by accident really. You see, we were playing in the woods when Jo suddenly disappeared into the ground. When we investigated, we found it was a flight of steps leading down into a tunnel."

Mr. MacBride looked puzzled. "But why wasn't the

entrance discovered when the woods were searched? And if you went down into the tunnel by a flight of steps, why didn't you come back that way?"

"We couldn't," said Jon shortly. "There was an iron grille, and Gonzales lowered it and locked it from his side. We had to try another way or stay there."

"Gonzales probably went to conceal the entrance when he left us alone. He wouldn't want anyone else walking in on him," Joanna commented.

"Yes, well, you're safe now, both of you," said Mrs. Mackenzie. "But please don't go anywhere else on your own."

Mr. Mackenzie looked serious. "Things seem to be coming to a head pretty fast now. They aren't going to threaten forever, you know. Pretty soon they'll come out into the open, and then. . . .well, anything might happen. I want to know where you two are all the time from now on."

"You're not treating it as a practical joke then, like the police suggest?" said Alistair MacBride.

"No, I'm not," Mr. Mackenzie replied, rather shortly. "It's gone beyond the bounds of practical joking. I'm taking it seriously, and I have advised the police accordingly."

There was an uncomfortable silence for a few moments, then Dr. Gordon reached across the table to help himself to some cheese. "Well, you two can't say you're not having an eventful holiday," he said with a smile.

"No, that we can't," Joanna replied. "Too eventful in some ways. We're just hoping to see the end of the mystery before we have to go back to school."

"Oh, I'm sure it will be solved before long," said

Alistair MacBride. "After all, this is only a small island. Gonzales can't remain hidden for ever. And someone must be keeping him supplied with food."

"Exactly—but who?" asked Mrs. Mackenzie.

"Ah, if you knew that, the mystery would no doubt be solved," was the non-committal answer.

"Dr. Gordon," said Jon, after a short pause, "are there any castles on the island?"

"Castles? Well, let's see now. There's the ruins of Inchnamur on the north east corner. It guarded the entrance to the channel, and is only a few ruins now. It might be worth a visit. Any particular reason?"

"Well, I have to do a holiday project on castles in the area," said Jon, "and I wondered if there are any hereabouts. I've found out something about Dunvegan in Skye."

"Pity Hamish isn't here," said Dr. Gordon. "He was a great authority on Scottish castles, and had visited most of them. Have you noticed the magnificent oil painting of Inverary Castle in the library? Done by a friend of his many years ago. Quite valuable, I believe. I know Hamish turned down a good offer for it some years before his death."

"Come on, Jo, let's go and look at it. Thanks, Dr. Gordon. You've been a big help."

The twins hurried off to the library. Before opening the door, Jon turned to his sister. "Don't say anything important in there, Jo. Remember the secret room. Someone may be listening."

He turned the door handle and went in. Everything was still and quiet. The rays of the setting sun were casting great swaths of golden red across the gently moving waves in the bay. The sudden switching on of the electric light darkened the gardens outside, and Jo moved across to close the heavy curtains.

Jon looked around the room. There were a number of fine paintings on the walls, but on a small section between two large bookcases was the painting of Inverary Castle.

"What a beautiful picture, Jo," said her brother. "The artist has really captured the beauty of the setting. Just look at the reflection of the castle in the waters of Loch Fyne."

"Yes, the colors are gorgeous. Who was the artist?"

Jon leaned forward to look in the corner of the picture, at the same time running his hand around the edge.

"Man named Lachlan. Come on, Jo, let's go upstairs now and finish that old castle project."

Nothing more was said until the twins reached the privacy of Jon's bedroom.

"You're being a bit mysterious, aren't you, Jon? Did you think that Gonzales might be listening?"

"It's just possible. There's no harm in being careful, and I don't want anyone to know what we've discovered this time."

"What we've discovered? Do you mean the code?"

"No," said her brother, very seriously. "What we discovered just now. Jo, there's a safe behind that picture of Inverary Castle, and that's where Don Alvarez's diary is hidden!"

9
The Diary of Don Alvarez

Breakfast next morning was a strain for the twins. Neither had slept particularly well, fearing that someone might discover the secret of the code and the hidden safe before they had examined its contents. Jon had counseled keeping their secret until after breakfast. Now the twins were waiting while Mr. Mackenzie downed his second cup of coffee. Finally, Jon could stand it no longer.

"Dad," he said quietly, but his voice was bubbling with excitement, "we've something to tell you and Mom."

"I thought you might have," said his father, grinning. "Come on then, don't keep us in suspense—let's have it."

"We've cracked the code and discovered the diary," Joanna blurted out, "at least. . . ."

"We know where the diary is, Dad," Jon interrupted, "but we wanted you and Mom to be there when we opened the safe."

He took a small piece of paper from his pocket and handed it across the table.

"This is the breakdown of the code message. The safe

79

is hidden behind the picture of Inverary Castle in the library. We found that out last night."

"Why didn't you come and tell us then?" asked their mother, looking puzzled.

"We didn't want Dr. Gordon and Mr. MacBride to know anything about it," said Jon. "I'm pretty sure that someone we trust is a traitor, and until we know who it is, I vote we don't trust anyone."

"But surely you don't think it could be either of Hamish's old friends?" said Mr. Mackenzie in a shocked voice.

Jon looked a bit defiant. "I don't know, Dad, but someone always knows all our plans and—to put it bluntly—I don't think it's Jamie or his mother, which leaves only Dr. Gordon and Mr. MacBride. I think we should be careful—very careful now that the secret is almost within our grasp."

"Perhaps you're right, Jon—we'll keep it to ourselves for the moment, anyway. Come on then, what are we hanging around for?"

He jumped to his feet and made for the door. As he was about to open it, Jon caught his arm.

"Dad! If the diary is there, bring it back here to look at it. There's a peephole to the library from a secret room, and someone—Gonzales—may be listening. In here we can't be overheard."

His father nodded gravely, and they all four hurried across to the library. Reaching the picture of Inverary Castle, Jon felt along the righthand side until his fingers discovered the hidden catch. With a slight click the picture swung away to reveal a small combination safe. Mr. Mackenzie looked at the paper in his hand and then dialed the figures—twenty left, seven right, six left—and the safe door swung open silently. Putting his hand inside, he withdrew two small volumes, one leather-bound and the other an ordinary hard-covered notebook. He closed the safe door, twisted the lock, replaced the picture, and beckoned to his family to follow him back to the breakfast room.

He placed the books on the table and looked at his wife with a wry grin. "What it is to have clever children!"

Jon's excitement bubbled over. "Let's see it, Dad!" He grabbed the leather-bound book. It was in beautifully tooled, red morocco leather. On the front cover, embossed in gold, was an intricate design, consisting of a heraldic shield with initials intertwined around it. Jon opened the book and leafed through the pages. All were covered in small italic writing.

"It's all in Spanish!" he said in disgust.

His parents laughed. "What did you expect, Jon? This—" his father indicated the second book, "I should imagine, is Uncle Hamish's translation."

He opened the book, and sure enough the flyleaf carried the heading: "Translation of the diary of Don Alvarez Jose Santamaria del Correo."

"It will take days to read," said Mrs. Mackenzie.

"I don't propose we should read it all now," said her husband, "but let's look at the end part in the hope that it will shed some light on the mystery."

He flicked the pages over, scanning paragraphs here and there. "Ah! Now this looks more like it." He began to read extracts from the different entries:

"*21st July, 1588*. Action today when the English fleet came out from Plymouth. Pedro de Valdez, commander of the Andalusian squadron, was captured. Beating up channel against strong wings.

"*23rd July, 1588*. Another battle off Portland. Many ships from both fleets damaged. Men tired and disheartened.

"*25th July*. Prolonged action off Isle of Wight. At darkness we beat a retreat to Calais.

"*27th July*. Admiral Medina Sidonia sent a message to Parma requesting immediate help, but Parma cannot sail because of the blockade.

"*28th July*. The English fleet sent fireships into Calais Roads. Our captains panicked and there was complete chaos as many ships cut loose their anchors and tried to put to sea.

"*29th July*. Great battle off Gravelines—the fiercest yet. Our Great Armada is no more. We have been battered and broken by the smaller ships of the English fleet, and all we can do now is try to get home to Spain. The weather is bad, and we are beating northwards along the coast of Belgium in heavy seas and strong winds.

"*30th July*. We are well past Nieuport but in danger of being driven on to a lee shore as we are unable to rig any spare anchors. The sea increased in fury during the night, and we were driven even further north. The English fleet followed us, but like us they have little food and no ammunition. Have ordered sail to be shortened. Cannot risk losing our topsails so far from home. Our only hope now is to beat around the north of Scotland."

Mr. Mackenzie scanned through a few more pages while the twins sat open-mouthed.

"*7th August.* At first light we sighted an island and a rocky coastline in the distance. Wind at gale force. Men very tired, many sick, particularly among the troops. Currents very treacherous here. No maps this far north, but it must be Scotland. Am going to try to beat around the coast. May be able to obtain food supplies from the natives as we go south.

"*8th August.* Position worsening. Sprang a leak during the night, and the men are working continuously to keep the water level down. Men in mutinous state, but we cannot heave to in this sea. Being swept towards coast. Do not think we can survive this time unless we can beach the ship somewhere to repair the leaks."

"Then there is a break of several days," Mr. Mackenzie reported.

"*11th August.* Yesterday we found ourselves in high seas off a small island. We tried to tack around the treacherous coast, but the current was too strong. We struck the rocks about six this morning, but I managed to bring her about and we did not appear badly damaged. Don Alonzo, my second in command, volunteered to take a line ashore by small boat so that the men could get off the *San Salvador* before she struck again. The seas were terrible, but as there was no alternative—only death for us all—I gave orders to launch the longboat, this being the strongest. The men landed safely, and Don Alonzo fastened the line firmly, signaling to the ship by waving his jacket from the top of a rocky promontory. I eased the *San Salvador* as close in as I dared, and the men swung themselves hand over hand down the line. Some, I fear, were lost, but many reached land safely. I could see them huddled together on the beach. As the last man, apart from Don Leon de Ferrara, my troop commander, and myself, left the ship, the rope broke. The men on the line were swept away, and a mountainous sea lifted the *San Salvador* like a leaf and tossed her down into a deep trough. I thought she would never come up again. I was thrown into the drain at the edge of the deck, but managed to cling on as a torrent of water poured over me. Don Leon was less fortunate. He was thrown against the mainmast and I fear his back is broken. It will be a miracle if we survive this night."

"Poor Don Alvarez," murmured Joanna. "He must have been a very brave man."

"But he was a Spaniard!" exclaimed Jon with some surprise.

"He was still a brave man," said his sister, gently.

"The next entry is dated the next day," their father continued.

"*12th August.* The end has come—for me and for the *San Salvador.* We stayed afloat during the night, to my surprise, for we seemed to be leaking badly. With daylight I could see the seas were even more mountainous and the wind was howling through the rigging like the Devil himself. I knew it was only a matter of time. An island loomed out of the morning mist—rocky and unfriendly looking. Whether it was the same island where my men landed I do not know. The cliffs were high and rugged, and laced with deep, black caverns. The current was dragging us in relentlessly, and the jagged rocks appeared hungry for our timbers. As I struggled to hold the wheel, I saw behind me a towering wave—fifty feet high or more. As it curled over the ship, I swung her bow around to point toward one of the caves. The wave hurled us forward like a little toy. The cave entrance was wide and high, and the *San Salvador* was thrust right inside, her mast-tops snapping off like twigs with the force. I was knocked to the deck by the wave, but my ship was firmly wedged inside the cave, unaffected by the tremendous undertow. When I recovered my senses, I realized that our bow was jammed in a rock crevice from which there is no exit. Even at low tide the heavy seas still pound right into the cave. My beautiful *San Salvador* is prisoner, settling gradually into the sand and rocks. Neither she nor I will ever sail again.

"*13th August*. Don Leon died in agony this forenoon. His cries were pitiful to hear, but there was nothing I could do to alleviate his suffering. God rest his soul.

"*14th August*. Much of the food is ruined by seawater. There is little left. The noise of the pounding waves and the darkness are getting on my nerves. There is no way out of the cave up the cliff because of the protruding overhang. I feel I am going mad. Oh, for the sound of a human voice!

"*15th August*. Today I made my decision. I found an intact barrel of gunpowder in the hold, unaffected by the water. Climbing to the high stern of the ship I clambered on to the rock at the cave entrance, and laid charges in the overhang and surrounding rocks. I lit the fuse from my tinderbox and took hasty refuge in my cabin. The noise of the explosion was deafening and seemed endless. At last I ventured out to see if my plan had been successful. The falling rocks had completely sealed the end of the cave—there was no vestige of daylight remaining, and even the sound of the sea was silenced. This will be our tomb—mine and the *San Salvador*. No one knows we are here—perhaps they will never know. I have done my best. The treasure entrusted to me to further the Catholic cause in our conquest of England is safe, and will be buried forever with me. May God forgive me for what I am about to do, but He knows I have no choice. I put my trust in Jesus whom I have loved all my life, and I know He will understand. Amen."

There was silence as Mr. Mackenzie finished reading. "Poor man—and, so you said, Joanna, a very brave one."

Both Joanna and her mother were unashamedly wiping their eyes.

"Isn't there any more?" asked Jon in a disappointed voice.

"Yes, there is a note from Uncle Hamish." His father read on, his voice reflecting the excitement that was so evident in the faces of his audience.

"This is a very free translation in modern language of the diary of Don Alvarez. How I came by it I will now tell you. This house—or part of it—dates back to about

1580. It got the name *'San Salvador'* from the fact that timbers bearing this name were washed up on the beach, and the then owner liked the name. The story of a treasure ship has been bandied around for centuries, and was presumed to have foundered in the bay during one of the worst storms ever known. I, too, have done my share of searching for it.

"Then one day I conceived the idea of building my own private air-raid shelter. In the last war I had used the cellars which are deep and dry, but with the advent of atomic weapons, I decided something more substantial was necessary. I blasted a large hole in the solid rock which formed one wall of the cellar, intending to chip it level, and then line it with concrete and steel. I was working on this one day when there was a sudden rumble, and I found myself half buried in rubble. When the dust cleared away and I managed to extricate myself, I saw some wood like a ship's mast jutting through a hole in the rock way above my head. I carefully enlarged the hole until I was able to squeeze through. With the aid of a lamp, I saw that I was in a huge cavern, and there, in front of me, was a galleon, her masts snapped short, but virtually intact. With great difficulty I managed to climb up the side until at last I stood on the deck. The silence and darkness were intense. In the large stern cabin, I found all that remains of Don Alvarez. In one hand was the diary, and in the other a dueling pistol.

"Later I searched the hold, and it is filled with Spanish treasure—gold and silver utensils, jewels, religious relics—even as Don Alvarez says. The ship is in a wonderful state of preservation, undoubtedly due to the fact that it has been completely sealed for so long.

"I abandoned my plans for the shelter, but procured a heavy steel door which I fitted to the entrance to the cavern. What was I to do with my secret? How to dispose of this tremendous treasure? All sorts of plans ran through my mind. I couldn't resist taking three gold pieces from one of the treasure chests and showing them to my friends, telling them that I found them washed up on a nearby beach. This was a mistake, and through this stupid act, the story soon got around that there was treasure to be found. I was badgered by phone calls and letters from would-be treasure seekers. Though some may have believed that I had already found the treasure myself, no one, I am sure, remotely suspected the real truth.

"Shortly after this discovery, I was stricken with arthritis, and became virtually a prisoner in my own house. I realized that the joy of announcing this discovery to the world would best be left to my successors, which is why I have indulged in these 'theatrical tricks.' What you do with the treasure, Andrew (for I am sure you will manage to solve the various little puzzles I have set), is up to you, but please, if my wishes carry any weight with you, use it in the following ways:

(1) For the upkeep and enhancement of the 'San Salvador' estate, which I have loved all my life, and for the benefit of your own family.
(2) To improve the situation of the islanders, who have always been my friends.
(3) For some fitting memorial to Don Alvarez, a

brave man and one for whom I felt much sympathy.

"To me has fallen the distinction of finding the greatest treasure since Tutankhamun's tomb was opened, but to you, Andrew, falls the glorious privilege of making this discovery known to the world.

"May God richly bless you and your family in your handling of this charge.

Hamish Mackenzie"

There was complete silence, and everyone seemed lost for words.

Then—"Can we—may we go and see it, Dad?" whispered Joanna.

Mr. Mackenzie picked up the books. "I'll just return these to the safe. I expect the key to the steel door is on Great-Uncle Hamish's key ring."

A few minutes later, the four of them were standing in the cellar.

"I can't see a steel door anywhere," said Jon, shining his flashlight around.

"No," said Mr. Mackenzie, "but that wooden framework may hide it."

A large wooden cupboard stood against the wall. Jon and his father heaved it to one side, revealing an opening, set deep inside of which was the steel door. They quickly opened it, and found themselves in a narrow passage which led through to the ship. Hamish had fixed a ladder to the side of the *San Salvador* so that it was a simple matter to reach the deck. Joanna gave a gasp of dismay when they entered the Captain's cabin and saw the huddled figure still bending over his desk, the jeweled gun still clasped by bony fingers.

Her father gripped her arm. "Don't be frightened, Jo. He's beyond everything now, except our sympathy and respect. We'll see he has a Christian burial."

They descended the ship's ladders to the hold, where everything was a complete shambles. But in a central compartment, completely unharmed, lay the treasure. The light from their flashlights sparkled on chests of jewels, gold and silver utensils, drinking goblets, cruc-ifixes and gold coins—a king's ransom. They stood and stared.

Then Mr. Mackenzie said quietly, "Come, let's go and inform the police. We shall need a guard over this until it can be listed and moved to a place of safety."

Speechless with wonder, they followed him back to the deck and down the ship's side to the cellar.

As Mr. Mackenzie turned to relock the door, two figures slid out of the shadows.

"I'll take that key, Andrew. You'll not be needing it now that you've shown me where the treasure's to be found."

They all spun around, to find themselves gazing into the barrels of two guns, held by Gonzales and—Alistair MacBride!

10

The End of the Holiday

Joanna gasped with fright and shrank back close to her father.

MacBride's smile of triumph struck fear into their hearts.

"You! Oh no—not you," stammered Mr. Mackenzie.

"Yes, me," said MacBride, grinning. "Why are you so surprised, Andrew? It had to be someone who knew old Hamish pretty well."

"But you were his friend! He always thought so highly of you."

"More fool he! I knew he'd found something, but I could never get him to discuss it. It wasn't for want of trying."

He whipped around as Jon made a move toward the door. "Get back there, you. Yes, it's a real gun I'm holding, and I won't hesitate to use it if you give me any more trouble. Hamish could have shared the treasure with me, but he was too mean—now I'm going to take it all!"

"Oh, no, you're not!" shouted Jon, angrily.

"And who's going to stop me? Not you, you young

whippersnapper! You've caused me enough trouble already." He pushed Jon back against the wall with his left hand, and brandished the gun in Mr. Mackenzie's face.

"The key—and make it quick. I want to get the treasure loaded and away before anyone suspects that something's up."

"What—what is going to happen to us?" Mrs. Mackenzie's voice trembled as she asked the question.

"You don't expect me to let you go, do you? To tittle-tattle to the police and set them on my trail? No, you will be locked in the cave when we've finished. It'll take you quite a while to dig yourselves out of there."

"But that's inhuman!" gasped Mrs. Mackenzie. "At least let the children go."

"The children! That's really funny! They've been the cause of all our troubles with their nosing around. Let them go! That's the last thing I'd do. Come on now—the key—or else I'll just have to shoot you and take it." MacBride waved the gun again, and Mr. Mackenzie, with a desperate look first at his son and then at his wife, held out the key.

"No, Dad—don't!" gasped Jon, but MacBride grabbed it, exultantly, even as Jon spoke.

As he turned towards the steel door, Gonzales pushed the four of them roughly against the wall. When the door opened, MacBride motioned with the gun. "Come on, now. Lead the way. And no tricks—there's too much at stake."

Mr. Mackenzie led the way, and despondently they climbed the ladder leading to the deck of the galleon.

"The treasure! Where's the treasure?" snarled Mac-Bride, jabbing the gun into Jon's ribs.

"Below—in the hold," gasped Joanna, as she saw Jon's face twist with sudden pain. They stumbled down the ladder into the hold, where Gonzales guarded them while MacBride played the light over the treasure. He knelt and dipped his hands greedily into the nearest chest, letting a scintillating cascade of jewels trickle through his fingers. They danced and sparkled in a myriad of different colors in the lantern light.

"Look at it!" MacBride whispered. "A king's ransom, and it's all mine. Fancy that stupid old fool sitting on a fortune and not telling anyone about it—he must have been mad!"

"Not as mad as you if you think you'll get away with this," said Jon, hotly taking a step forward.

"Back!" snarled Gonzales, and Mr. Mackenzie reached out quickly and drew his son back against the bulkhead.

"How shall we shift this stuff, boss?" asked Gonzales.

"We'll tie them up first and then we'll be free to get on with it," said MacBride. "We'll shift it outside first, and seal the door again. Then we'll move it to the yacht. We don't want to run the risk of someone getting away and giving the alarm."

Gonzales drew some rope from his pocket, and it took only moments to fasten the Mackenzie family securely.

"Ye'll not leave us tied up when you've finished?" ask Andrew Mackenzie.

"What difference will it make?" asked MacBride. "You won't be able to get out."

Gonzales gave a shout of laughter.

93

Mr. Mackenzie struggled with the ropes.

"All right, take it easy," said MacBride. "I'll untie you before I go. I can afford to be generous."

He and Gonzales began transporting everything of value from the galleon. It took quite a long time, and the Mackenzie family watched helplessly. Jon was seething with rage, and his father could not resist a smile as he saw the tears in his son's eyes.

"Steady now, son. Getting angry won't do any good. Jesus said, 'Lay not up for yourselves treasure upon the earth. . . .' MacBride will not benefit from this treasure—you'll see."

"But Dad—" Jon checked himself and bit his lip hard to check the tears. "You're right, of course, Dad, but it's hard to see them taking all the treasure and not to be able to do anything about it."

"Especially when they only found it because of us," Joanna exclaimed, hotly.

"I wonder how they knew we'd found it ," said her brother.

"That's easily answered, son" MacBride said, pausing on the ladder. "A small microphone in the breakfast room told us all we needed to know."

"You thief!" said Jon, angrily, and MacBride's laughter floated down the compainionway.

"What can we do, Andrew?" asked Mrs. Mackenzie, quietly.

"Only pray, dear. I'm certain that our good Lord is aware of our plight, and has the matter in hand. We can do nothing in our own strength at the moment, so we must trust Jesus to help us."

There was a shuffling sound on the ladder as Mac-

Bride descended again into the hold, and stood in front of his captives.

"We have taken all we want," he said, "so now we will leave you to enjoy your inheritance." He reached to take the lantern off the hook, then paused. "Perhaps I will leave the light so that you can enjoy the beauties of your prison. It will probably last long enough." He laughed mirthlessly, and Joanna shivered.

MacBride went towards the ladder.

Mr. Mackenzie pulled frantically against the ropes. "MacBride!" he shouted. "You promised to cut us free!"

MacBride half turned, the lantern throwing an enormous ugly shadow against the bulkhead. "So—I am a liar as well as a thief. It's too dangerous to set you free. No one will ever find you in time to incriminate me—if they find you at all. Adios, amigos. Enjoy the time that is left to you."

With a brief wave of his hand he was gone.

Jon groaned and his head drooped forward in despair. The light flickered across their faces—Mrs. Mackenzie's taut with unspoken anxiety; Joanna's wide-eyed with ill-concealed fear; her father's rigid with anger.

"Do you think perhaps—Jamie might—?" hazarded Mrs. Mackenzie.

"We can only hope, but we mustn't count on it. We must try to get free," replied her husband. "Come on now. We're not dead yet. Don't give up. Any chance of getting your hands free?"

Even Jon perked up, and they all began struggling with their ropes. After a long time, there was an excited

95

cry from Joanna. "I've done it! I've managed to wriggle one hand out!"

"Good for you, Jo," said her brother, brightening up considerably.

It took only a few minutes for Joanna to free the others.

"What now, Dad?" Jon took the lantern off its hook and shone it around. Mr. Mackenzie's keen eyes spotted a rusty crowbar lying in one corner. He grabbed it and made for the ladder.

"See if you can find anything else that can be used for digging," he said over his shoulder. "And hurry!"

Quickly they searched around, and before long each had found something suitable, and joined Mr. Mackenzie back at the steel door. They found him searching the sides of the cave entrance with a tiny pencil flashlight.

"Let's have the lantern over here, Jon," he called. Jon quickly held the lantern up, letting the light fall on the rock face.

"Joanna!"

"Yes, Dad?"

"Can you squeeze under the bowsprit and try the rock there? Jon and I will work this side. Myra, you hold the lantern and relieve us when one of us gets tired."

They quickly got to work, prying at the rock with the ancient tools they had found. Soon dust and rock chips were flying through the air.

"Dad! I thought I felt this piece give a little."

Jon attacked it furiously, while his father took a brief rest. Then suddenly the rock gave, and Jon fell on his face in the dust. His mother held the lantern to shine through the hole, which looked quite deep.

Jon and his father started to enlarge the opening. "I believe I could crawl through there now," Jon said. "It must lead to the cellar, and if I can climb through here, I can probably manage to break through the other end. It can't be far."

"It's worth a try," said his father, "but be careful."

Jon eased himself into the hole, and started to jab at the rock with his crowbar, passing the pieces out behind him.

After a while, "I'm through to the cellar," he called, "and I can see—it's Jamie! Jamie!" he screamed.

"Can he help us, Jon?" called his father.

There was a flurry of loose rock and Jon scrambled back.

"Thank God!" said Mrs. Mackenzie, fervently.

"Our prayers have certainly been answered, my dear," said her husband.

The waiting seemed endless, but at last they heard the click of the lock as the massive steel door was opened, and a sudden shaft of bright light blinded them.

They stumbled out into the cellar, to be confronted by Jamie, Mrs. Sinclair, Inspector Reid, and two policemen.

"MacBride?" stammered Mr. Mackenzie, grabbing at the Inspector's arm.

"On his way to the police station, sir. And Gonzales, too," said the Inspector. "Are you all right?"

"Yes," gasped Joanna. "What happened?"

Jamie caught her arm as she staggered slightly.

"I saw Gonzales in the woods early this morning," said Jamie, "and then I spotted MacBride's yacht in the bay under the headland. I've had my doubts about yon MacBride for some time, so I called Inspector Reid, and we watched what was happening. When we saw them carrying chests out of the cellar and down to the yacht, we knew something was up."

"Was there a fight?" asked Jon, excitedly.

"We took them by surprise," said the Inspector, "but MacBride was so angry that he went berserk, and it took three of us to hold him down while we got the handcuffs on him. He wouldn't say anything, of course, but Gonzales was only too ready to spill the beans, and we soon found the key in MacBride's pocket."

"Was Gonzales really a Spaniard?" asked Mrs. Mackenzie.

The Inspector laughed. "No. His name was Joe Bloggs from the East End of London—a second-rate actor MacBride hired specially for the job."

"I would miss all the fun," grumbled Jon.

"You're not doing so badly," said the Inspector. "I'll have to take statements from you about what has happened."

"All in good time, Inspector—we've got something to show you first," said Mr. Mackenzie. "Follow me, all of you."

* * * * * * *

The last night before the end of the summer holiday found the Mackenzie family seated in the lounge after dinner, together with Dr. Gordon and Inspector Reid. The door opened and Mrs. Sinclair came in with the coffee, followed by her son.

"Ah, coffee," said Mr. Mackenzie. "Put it on this table, Mrs. Sinclair, and come and sit down. You too, Jamie. Joanna will do the honors."

Joanna obediently got up, poured and passed around the coffee.

"I've asked Mrs. Sinclair and Jamie to join us," explained Mr. Mackenzie, "because they are directly concerned with the plans I've made for the 'San Salvador' estate."

They all looked at him expectantly.

"There's been plenty of publicity," said Jon. "We've been in all the papers. Just wait till we get back to school, Jo. We'll have something to tell them."

"Yes," said his father. "We've certainly been in the limelight. Well now, I've been to my lawyers, who tell me that there has to be a Coroner's Inquest over any treasure trove discovered—that is, gold and silver—to establish whether there is a rightful owner. Then it is handed over to the Crown, and experts from the British Museum assess its value—a very substantial amount indeed in this case, and there is no doubt that, as owner of the estate, this money will come to me."

"Then we're going to be rich," gasped Joanna.

"Well—yes, we are," said Mr. Mackenzie, "but let me tell you our plans.

"Part of the sum will be set aside for each member of the family and for Mrs. Sinclair and Jamie, and a further part for the benefit of the islanders. The remainder will be put into a fund administered by a small committee including, if they will agree, Dr. Gordon and Inspector Reid. This fund will enable 'San Salvador' to be run as a children's holiday home, of which Mrs. Sinclair will be matron, and Jamie will be responsible for the upkeep of the estate. Here, deprived children from Glasgow and other cities can come, not only for a healthy holiday, but also to learn of the love of Jesus and the salvation that is ours by believing in Him. We can start work on plans for this even before the legal side is settled."

"But where will we live?" Jon burst out. "We're surely not going back to London!"

Mrs. Mackenzie laughed. "No," she said. "We like it here too much for that. But the house is really way too big just for us, so we're going to have a smaller place built on the headland. The view is magnificent up there. We thought we might call it 'Santamaria' after Don Alvarez."

"What will happen to the galleon?" asked Joanna.

"I've some experts coming to see it soon. They will advise whether any special requirements are necessary to preserve it. It is quite unique, and if all goes well, we could make it into a sort of museum—a permanent tribute to Don Alvarez."

"That would be nice," murmured Joanna. "Poor man, I feel so sorry for him."

"Well now," said Mr. Mackenzie, "is everyone in agreement with these ideas?" He smiled across at the children.

"I think it's a marvelous idea, Dad, and just what Great-Uncle Hamish would have done, I should think," said Jon.

"Well, if you all agree, I don't think we need keep you children any longer. You must have things to do as you're off to school tomorrow. I hope you have your holiday projects finished by now."

The twins nodded and said goodnight.

* * * * * * *

Jon and Joanna made their way up to the headland in silence. The moon was bright, and the night clear and still.

"It'll be lovely to have a house just here," said Joanna, at length. "This is my favorite spot."

"Mine, too," said her brother. "Perhaps they'll be well on with the building by the time we are here again."

"I hope so," murmured Joanna. "Oh, Jon, how I shall miss 'San Salvador'—and you, of course," she added, hastily.

"Yes," Jon agreed. "This holiday has been an eye-opener for me in more ways than one. Last night I decided to accept Jesus as my personal Savior. I read the passages of Scripture you gave me, and God certainly opened my eyes and understanding. I asked Jesus to forgive all my sins, and to help me to keep His commandments. It won't be easy I know, and no doubt the other boys will make fun of me, but if I trust Jesus, I know He will help me. I've come to think differently about prayer since I've seen it in action so effectively."

"Prayer *does* work, Jon. Try not to forget that."

"I won't. Say, Joanna—do you know what I could do with right now? A couple of Mrs. Sinclair's delicious scotch pancakes dripping with oodles of butter."

"Och aye, laddie, ye canna be hoongry again," said Joanna with a grin, in a broad imitation of Mrs. Sinclair.

"I am that—talking always makes me hungry," he replied with a laugh. "Race you to the kitchen," and he took off down the headland path into the deepening shadows.

Joanna paused as the path dropped down towards the house, knowing that the *San Salvador* itself lay almost beneath her feet.

"Good-by, Don Alvarez. Rest in peace," she whispered, and hurried after the fast disappearing figure of her brother.